Enchanting the Innkeeper

LOVE IN APPLE BLOSSOM
BOOK FIVE

KIT MORGAN

Enchanting the Innkeeper

(Love in Apple Blossom, Book 5)

© 2023 Kit Morgan

Cover design by Angel Creek Press and EDH Designs

❀ Created with Vellum

License Note

Chapter One

Phileas Darlington was a practical sort. But when he heard his brother Wallis tell Jean Campbell, Apple Blossom's town undertaker, at the town dance that he was in love with her and asked her to marry him, he became very impractical indeed.

Phileas stumbled from the grassy dance area into the darkness beyond the torchlight. He had to think! Though what was there to think about other than helping Dora Jones with her hotel, then going home to England? But—and it was a *big* but—what if he didn't make it? First his brother Sterling had succumbed to love's lure with Letty Henderson. Then Conrad fell, followed by Irving. And now poor Wallis was besotted with the undertaker of all people. What would become of them?

A better question was, what would become of his

family's estate back in England? Phileas and his brothers were in America on holiday—one last great adventure before their mother put them on the marriage mart. Once that happened, their lives would be over. She'd have them married off to the best of the best as far as she was concerned. Love had nothing to do with it. Positions, power, and a good-sized dowry from each bride were all that mattered to her. That and getting herself some grandchildren.

Phileas ran his hand through his hair. They'd been in Apple Blossom mere weeks and now four of his brothers were getting married. What if none of them returned? The title and estate would fall to him and, like the rest of his brothers sans Sterling the eldest, he didn't want it. For one, it was a lot of work. Besides, he was an artist and had found his calling amidst all the decorating he'd been doing since his arrival in the little town. Now he had his chance to really create something special with the hotel, but this? Oh, dash it all, he might never get the chance now.

He paced, trying to come up with a plan. He'd still do the hotel; it might be his last chance to create a work of beauty. Once his mother and father got hold of him and stuffed his head full of facts and figures and everything that went into running a grand estate, he'd have to say goodbye to his artistic endeavors for good. What a horrid thought!

"What are you doing here, lurking in the dark?" a woman snapped.

He sighed as his shoulders slumped. "Good evening, Mrs. Featherstone. I might ask the same of you." He turned around and could just make out her face. As usual, she wore a pinched expression that made her look as if her shoes were too tight or she'd just eaten a lemon.

"That's none of your concern. Get back to the party." Agnes Featherstone moved past him and into the torchlight.

He watched her go and sighed. "Things could be worse, chap. You might have to marry something like that." He shuddered at the thought and went back to the throng of townspeople as they laughed, danced, ate, and made merry. The dance was the first in Apple Blossom in a long time and the residents were taking advantage of it. They'd suffered a tragedy some months back and lost a lot of loved ones.

Phileas supposed he and his brothers stumbling upon the town was a godsend for the tiny community, and they'd been there ever since. But their time was running short, and his brothers would have to decide whether they were going home or staying here.

He went to a chair and sat. His brothers were all dancing—Sterling, Conrad, Irving, and Wallis with their respective betrothed, and Oliver, the youngest, with Mrs. Watson. Her precocious son Billy had been helping his brothers with their projects. He worked hard and was making money too.

His eyes drifted to Irving and Sarah Crawford. The young widow had two small children, so he didn't see

Irving returning to England. Conrad, second in line to inherit, was already working as the town deputy. His future wife, Sheriff Cassie Laine, was smiling at him. Wallis might return to England with Jean in tow, but Phileas hoped Sterling would come to his senses and go. He'd been groomed to take over the estate and title, and though Irving and Conrad were both capable, neither had the training their eldest brother had.

He slumped in his chair.

"What's the matter with you?"

Phileas looked up. Dora stood before him, hands on hips. She wore a green dress and had even styled her hair differently for the occasion. "Thinking."

"That's it? Thinking?" She sat beside him. "About Wallis and Jean?"

He crossed his arms. "Among other things."

She watched him a moment and said nothing. What could be going through her head? Then again, did he really want to know?

"I congratulated them," she finally said.

"Good for you." He looked her way. "Did my brother convey when he'd like to marry Miss Campbell?"

She laughed. "What is wrong with you? Since when do you call Jean 'Miss Campbell'? You've been using her first name almost since you got here."

He shrugged. "Just being formal." He looked her in the eyes. She had nice blue eyes. If he could find some velvet curtains in the same shade, he'd put them throughout the hotel.

"Well, I think it's wonderful," she said. "Stop being grumpy about it."

He sat up. "I am not grumpy." He stared straight ahead and realized he was frowning. He forced a smile and looked at her again.

"Nice try." She left the chair. "I'm going to get some punch—want some?"

He got to his feet. "I'll fetch it."

"Why? I was heading to the refreshment tables anyway."

"Because it's what a gentleman does." He bowed, then skirted the dance area to the tables at the far end. The musicians were at the other, a piano, fiddle and guitar. It wasn't much, but it served.

When he reached the tables, he spied Wallis and Jean holding hands and giving each other looks of admiration and affection. It made him want to run.

"Phileas," Wallis called. "Come join us."

Too late. He forced another smile and headed over. The sooner he got this over with the better. "Well, you two look happy."

"We are," Wallis said. "Come toast with us." He held up a glass of punch.

Phileas smiled again, this one more pathetic than the last, and reached for a glass. He filled it and held it up.

"To my future bride!" Wallis said happily. "May she put up with all my foibles."

"Do you have a lot?" Jean asked.

"More than you know," Phileas quipped. He

touched his glass to his brother's, then Jean's. "But you'll get used to them."

She giggled and sipped her punch.

Phileas took a drink, licked his lips and gazed across the dance area. He still had to bring Dora her punch. "If you'll excuse me, I have a thirsty lady to take care of."

Wallis smiled. "By all means." His eyes widened. "Oh, um, Dora?"

"Yes." Phileas filled a glass for her and started back. He heard Wallis say something but couldn't make it out. No matter – if it was anything important, he'd come after him.

Wallis didn't. Phileas sighed in relief and continued toward Dora. Tomorrow he'd get to work on the hotel and get as much of it done as he could before it was time for... well, whomever was willing to return to England to do so. He hoped it wasn't just himself and Oliver.

Speaking of Ollie, where was he? Mrs. Watson was playing the piano again and he couldn't spot his younger brother anywhere. Hmm, maybe he was using the privy.

He reached Dora, handed her the punch, then sipped his own.

"Thank you," she said and smiled.

Phileas nodded, then gazed at the townsfolk as they continued their revelry. He wished he could be happier, but his evening had been ruined. Was he happy for Wallis? Of course. Did he want to throttle him for falling in love? It was tempting. But dash it all, there was little he could do about it now except hope and pray that Sterling would come to his senses, marry Letty, then go home to England. If not, he was doomed.

§♠

Dora studied Phileas a moment, then stood. "I'm going to find Letty."

He glanced her way, sighed and nodded. She had no idea what was wrong with him, but she wasn't going to let him sour *her* evening. She wanted to dance and have fun, and by golly, she was going to do it.

She found Oliver speaking with Billy and some of the other children. "Where did Wallis and Jean get to?"

Billy pointed to somewhere beyond the torchlight. "I think they're sparking."

"Sparking, are they?" Dora took one look at Oliver and shook her head. "I didn't know Englishmen sparked."

Oliver's eyes lit up. "He's starting a fire?"

She covered her mouth to stifle a giggle. "Not exactly. And if he is, then I'd better go chaperone. Billy, where did you say they are?"

"They went thataway." He pointed at the dark once more.

She took a deep breath. She wasn't fond of dark places and less fond of wandering around in the night, but they couldn't be far away. She headed in the direction Billy indicated.

"Dora, wait." Oliver caught up to her. "You

shouldn't try to find them when you can't see." He offered her his arm. "You could trip."

She looked at his arm and nodded. "You're right." She took it and off they went.

"I hope you're not trying to find them because you think Wallis will take advantage of his newly betrothed status and do more than steal a few kisses."

"Not at all, but Agnes will spread all over town that they have to get married."

"Oh, that," Oliver groaned. "I hadn't thought that far ahead. You're right, of course."

"I know Agnes." She stopped them once they were shrouded in darkness. "Jean?"

They heard a giggle up ahead and to their right. "Ah, there they are," Oliver said.

She smiled and they headed that way. "Jean, you shouldn't be out here with Wallis. There's going to be talk."

Jean almost bumped into them, Wallis right behind her. "We already ran into Agnes, and she returned to the dance. Don't worry, my virtue is intact."

"We had no doubts," Oliver said. "But you two should return. Billy is busy telling everyone you're trying to start a fire out here."

"What?" Wallis glanced at Jean and back.

Dora smiled. "He told Oliver the two of you were *sparking*."

Jean flew into hysterics. "Oh, that's precious." She took one look at Oliver and laughed again.

"I say, did I do something wrong?" He scratched his head then sniffed at his clothes. "Is it me? I know I still smell but ..."

"It's not you," Dora said through her giggles. "If you don't know, sparking means kissing."

"Oh, I see," he said with a grin. "Ha! No wonder you were worried about my brother starting a fire." He started laughing, which only made Dora laugh harder. At least now she was having a good time. She wasn't sure what ruined Phileas' evening, but she would not let it ruin hers.

The four headed back to the dance area laughing and talking, and she wondered if they'd run into Phileas along the way. So far, she didn't see him. Had he left and gone back to the hotel?

They made their way to the refreshment tables and Dora got her first jab of disappointment. There was no sign of Phileas anywhere. "Have you seen Phileas? He seems to have disappeared."

Wallis and Oliver scanned the area as Jean filled glasses with punch. "Is he dancing?" she asked.

Wallis stood on tiptoe and craned his neck as he scanned the crowd. "I don't see him."

"That's odd," Oliver said. "Where could he be?"

Dora looked at the back of the hotel. "Perhaps he's had enough festivities for one evening."

Wallis and Oliver exchanged an odd look then followed her gaze. "Um, yes," Wallis said. "Perhaps so."

She looked at the food table and took a plate. "Is

9

anyone else hungry?" She grabbed a piece of fried chicken first, then spooned some fried potatoes onto the plate. She continued to pile things on and knew everything she was taking would appeal to Phileas. If he wasn't feeling well, he might still be hungry later. She'd made nothing for dinner because of the dance, so this would be the only snack he'd get.

"Someone's hungry," Jean commented as she filled her own plate.

"I'm taking this to the hotel. If Phileas is there, he might want some of this later. I hope he's not taken ill."

"Great Scott, don't suggest such a thing," Wallis said. "We need him."

"So do I." She glanced at the hotel again. "He's promised to do a lot of things to that hotel of mine, and I want to make sure he does."

Oliver smiled at her. "You love that old place, don't you?"

"I do and want to see it repaired. Phileas has a good eye and good ideas. The last thing I want is him sick in bed." With a parting nod she headed across the dance area. The musicians were taking a break and heading for the food, as were many of the townsfolk now.

She slipped away to the street and walked to the hotel. The boardwalk was lit by torches, so there was plenty of light to see her way. When she arrived, she went straight for the staircase. Phileas' door was open when she reached it, and she knocked on the door jamb.

He sat up. "Dora, what are you doing here?"

She held up the plate. "I brought you some food. I didn't want you getting hungry later. There's nothing for you to snack on downstairs."

He smiled and left the bed. "How thoughtful." He crossed the room and took the plate from her. "Thank you so much."

She smiled but did nothing to hide the concern in her eyes. "Are you okay? You don't have a fever, do you?"

"Good heavens, no. I'm... not in the mood for dancing this evening." He took the plate to the small desk in the corner. "Thank you for thinking of me."

Was he dismissing her? She clasped her hands in front of her and stepped into the room. "You're welcome." She stared at the floor, unsure what to say next. She didn't want to pry but knew something was wrong. "Everyone will ask after you. What should I tell them?"

He picked up a piece of chicken. "Tell them I'll return momentarily. If I don't, I'll not hear the end of it."

She smiled, nodded, and tried not to wring her hands. "Is it Wallis and Jean? Are you upset that..."

He waved the chicken leg at her. "It's nothing to be concerned with." He glanced around the room. "Don't worry, I'll still help you."

"Oh, no, it's not that." She waved the thought aside. "If you're able to work on the hotel, then wonderful, but don't think..."

"Dora, I said I'll still help you. You needn't worry."

She let her arms fall loose at her sides. "Thank you. It means a lot to me."

He smiled. "Well, it's not like anyone else could give it that special something, hm?"

She laughed. "No. Not the way you can." She took another step toward him. "I should go."

"If you wait a bit, I'll go with you." He took a generous bite of chicken.

She watched him eat and smiled.

He swallowed and smiled back. "Do have some. You brought plenty."

"I thought it would last you through tomorrow."

"Not if Oliver gets to it first."

She smiled again. Oliver was notorious for raiding the icebox in the middle of the night. "True." She sat in a chair by the door.

"You're not hungry?"

"I'll fix a plate when we return."

He ate faster.

"Please, take your time," she urged.

He pulled a handkerchief from his pocket and used it as a napkin. "Let's put this in the icebox and go. That way Oliver will have something to eat later."

She nodded and left the chair. "If that's what you'd like."

He picked up the plate and approached. "What I'd like is to share a meal with you and discuss what I'll do first with this place."

She sighed in relief and hoped he didn't think the hotel was the only reason she was here. "Thank you."

He bowed. "Never fear, fair maiden. I'm here to rescue you." He looked around again. "And your hotel."

Chapter Two

They returned to the dance after putting his food in the icebox, and Phileas raided the refreshment tables there. He loaded his plate with fried chicken, potatoes, pie, and an assortment of other goodies, all spread before him like a feast. He was trying to eat away his troubles, and while he knew it was a temporary solution, it was still worth the effort.

The food tasted like a dream, and soon he was lost in the music and dancing around him. He swayed to the rhythm of Woodrow Atkins' fiddle as he ate, feeling a strange fresh energy radiating through him. He knew it was just a momentary respite from his troubles, but for now it was enough.

Of course, what would really make him feel better was starting work on the hotel. Now there was a project, and he'd been champing at the bit to start, but every time he thought he could, he got pulled away to work on something else with one or all of his brothers.

Dora sat beside him with a full plate and picked at her food. Phileas should ask her to dance but didn't have it in him at the moment. If his brothers saw him dancing with Dora, would they panic? Would his heart getting caught in love's snare push them to the altar as fast as they could to say their I do's? Hmm, good thing he wasn't falling head over heels in love. He wasn't sure what his brothers would do.

He was just getting to his pie when Sterling and Letty approached. "Evening, Phileas," Sterling greeted. "Enjoying yourself?"

He looked up from his plate. "As much as expected, I suppose." He studied his immediate surroundings. "Is there something you want?"

Sterling smiled. "Nothing." His eyes fixed on Dora. "Are you having an enjoyable time?"

She swallowed some cake. "Oh, yes." She gave Phileas a sidelong glance. "Though I haven't danced yet."

Sterling bowed. "Then allow me?" He motioned to the dance area.

Dora smiled. "Don't mind if I do."

Letty laughed, took her plate from her and sat next to Phileas.

He watched Dora leave with Sterling with a pinch of jealousy. Now where did that come from? He took a large bite of apple pie, and the sweet cinnamon flavor burst across his taste buds. He sighed. Yes, something like this was worth living for.

He tried not to look as Dora and Sterling danced in the center of the grassy dance floor. Instead, he concentrated on the music through the loud conversations of the other townsfolk. He leaned back in his chair with a contented smile on his face and a plate of just the right amount of food in his hands. He might have indigestion tomorrow, but it was well worth it tonight. For all he knew, he was the next Viscount Darlington.

He started on his slice of cake as Sterling and Dora returned. Letty had kept things to idle chitchat and said not one word about Wallis and Jean. That meant Sterling was going to pull him aside and lecture him.

Sure enough, as soon as his brother reached him, Sterling gave him that all too familiar smile. "Phileas, walk with me."

He took one last look at his plate and sighed. "Oh, very well." He handed his plate to Letty, who was handing Dora's back to her. "Do you mind?"

Letty smiled. "Not at all, though I can't promise your cake will still be here when you return." She winked, then took a bite.

He eyed his brother then shook his head. "Just because she's now part of the family, doesn't mean she can help herself to what's on my plate."

Sterling put his arm around him. "Yes, it does." He steered him away from Letty and Dora.

"So, what do you want to talk about?"

Sterling said nothing at first and kept walking.

"Brother, you're making me nervous." Phileas chanced a glance at him. Sterling's face was stoic, void of emotion. This was going to be some talk.

Sterling stopped when they reached the back of Captain Stanley's saloon. "Phileas, this pains me to ask, but are you in love with Dora?"

Phileas blinked a few times before he burst out laughing. "What? Is that what you wanted to ask me?" He wiped a tear from his eye. "Oh, brother, you don't know how relieved I am. I thought you were going to ask me how I felt about having to take over the title and estate..." His face fell. "Are you?"

Sterling ran his hand through his hair. "I'm still torn. And, I admit, I fear being disinherited. You know it could happen."

He stared at him a moment. "Do you really think our parents would stoop so low?"

"Mother would in an instant if it meant saving face." He walked to the saloon's back porch. "Irving wants to let Sarah start a business, so she'll have a feeling of accomplishment. Can you imagine what Mother would say to Irving if he returned to England with Sarah and her children in tow?"

Phileas went to a bench on the porch and sat. "I've tried not to think about it."

"Well, she won't be happy, I can tell you that. And what about Conrad? Once she finds out he got himself a job as deputy—for a lady sheriff, no less—Mother will go through the roof."

"And Wallis?"

Sterling laughed. "He wants to marry an undertaker. What do you think?"

"Yes, I see your point."

"Do you?" Sterling left the porch and paced in front of it. "What I'm trying to say is, you can't fall in love." He looked Phileas in the eyes. "Please, brother, I mean it. The rest of us will muddle through. But you must think of Oliver."

Phileas gaped at him. "What does he have to do with this?"

"He's the youngest, the least experienced. It would take Father twice as long to teach him what he needs to know. But he can teach you in no time."

Phileas stood. "What are you saying?"

Sterling took a deep breath. "I'm saying that the title and estate are yours."

Phileas stepped back, hit the bench and fell onto it. "You jest."

"No. I've thought about it. I can't take Letty away from here. This is her home, and ... I've grown accustomed to this way of life."

Phileas jumped to his feet. "In a few weeks?!"

"I'm in love," Sterling said with a helpless shrug.

Phileas rolled his eyes and tossed his hands in the air. "So, it's fine for you to fall in love but not me?"

"No, I didn't mean it that way."

Phileas frowned. "Then what did you mean?"

Sterling sighed. "Just not to fall in love here."

He laughed. "Because our parents will disinherit the lot of us?"

"Yes."

Phileas exhaled and shook his head. "That's ridiculous. And for your information, I do not intend to fall in love in Apple Blossom."

Sterling nodded. "Good. Because if you did, you'd be putting the future of the family at risk."

Phileas fixed him with a gaze. "Don't worry, I understand. I won't do anything stupid."

Sterling nodded curtly. "Glad to hear it." He motioned to the dance. "Shall we return?"

Phileas stiffened. He could fall in love with whomever he chose. Yes, Sterling was trying to protect the estate and title, but blast it, if it was *his* heart they were talking about, would he be as cooperative?

They returned to the party, but Phileas felt a weight on his chest. He glanced at Dora with a sigh. No, he couldn't let himself fall in love, not here, not with her. He steeled himself and made his way to the punch bowl. With any luck, the night would fly by if he helped himself to another glass and more desserts.

By the time he returned to Dora and Letty, he managed to gulp down a couple of cookies and two glasses of punch. If this kept up, he'd have a bellyache come morning. But he was angry now. Why did he have to be the sacrificial lamb for their parents? And if, perchance, Father disinherited them, could Phileas just as easily put them back in good standing with their parents after some time passed?

He hoped so, because he would *not* run that big estate on his own.

❦

Dora watched Phileas at the food table and sighed. "One would think he's a bear preparing to hibernate."

Letty followed her gaze. "He seems quite hungry."

"Something's wrong," Dora observed. She didn't mean to draw attention by the comment and hoped Letty didn't say more. She didn't—Sterling joined them and whisked her away to the dance area.

Dora continued to watch Phileas as he loaded another plate and began to eat. He strolled toward Oliver, and she wondered if he would discuss with his younger brother whatever Sterling talked with him about.

At least poor Oliver didn't smell as bad as he had the last few days. After getting sprayed by a skunk while working on Sarah Crawford's house, he'd been sequestered in his room at the hotel hoping the smell would fade. Frequent baths helped, but the poor man had almost scrubbed his skin raw in the attempt to get rid of the odor before the town dance.

She pushed the thought from her mind and went toward the two men. If Sterling told Phileas his work on

20

the hotel would be delayed yet again, then didn't she have a right to know? It was her hotel, after all, and if Phileas didn't take care of business soon, he'd never get the chance. She could tell he was getting nervous, and wanted to do what she could to help him see this through. But his brothers weren't helping matters.

"... And so, I won't be falling in love anytime soon," Phileas was saying when she got within earshot.

She stopped short. Had anyone else heard? Dora studied their immediate surroundings. Mr. Watson was speaking to Alma Kirk the owner of the general store. Mr. Smythe was eating with his wife next to them. They seemed too engrossed in their conversation and food to pay Phileas and Oliver any mind.

Oliver chuckled low in his throat. "Was he joking?"

"No," Phileas said stoically. "I'm afraid he wasn't."

"That hardly seems fair," Oliver pointed out.

"Well, that's how it has to be." Phileas sighed and slapped Oliver on the back. "He's only doing what he thinks is best. He's worried about Mother and Father."

Oliver nodded sagely. "They'll disinherit him?"

Phileas nodded but said nothing.

Dora sidestepped the brothers and disappeared into the crowd. "What?" Had she heard them, right? She would think Sterling's parents would be happy he found a wife. Is that why he was considering staying in America? And what about Conrad and Irving? Were they thinking of doing the same only because they wouldn't be welcomed back in England? Were Mr. and Mrs.

Darling the sort that tried to control the lives of their children? Did they have others in mind to marry their sons off to?

Her hand went to her chest. What about Jean? Would they accept her? Would Wallis stay in Apple Blossom for the same reason?

She went to the row of chairs on one side of the dance area and sat. No one else occupied them which meant people were dancing or eating. No matter, she wanted to be alone to process this. From the sounds of it, Phileas and Oliver, as the only single sons remaining, were still in good standing with their parents. Therefore, they would return to England to help the parents run the farm. She knew it had to be big, but how big she still had no idea.

"Hi, Dora," came a familiar voice.

She smiled. "Hello, Billy. What are you doing?"

He sat next to her. "No one will dance with me."

"What?" she said with raised eyebrows. "Why ever not?"

He sighed. "I'm too short."

She laughed. "You're seven. You're not supposed to be tall yet."

"I know, but the older girls won't dance with me either and they're shorter than you."

She nodded. "I can see you have a problem. Tell you what, I'll dance with you."

His eyes lit up. "You will?"

"Sure." She left the chair and took Billy's hand. "Come on, let's go."

She led him into the middle of the dance area and stood before him. "Do you know how to dance?"

"Sure, my ma taught me this one." He took her hands in his and led her around. Everyone was doing a simple folk dance and thankfully she knew it too. Pa wasn't one for dancing and hadn't taught her much. What she knew, she'd learned from Letty and Cassie.

They danced by Phileas and Oliver, and she smiled as Billy did his best to keep up with her. He was the only child dancing. The others were playing hide and seek near the saloon.

Phileas smiled back and watched them until they disappeared into the rest of the dancers. Everyone made their way around the dance area in a big circle. There were smaller circles of people and every five turns, the outer circle switched with the inner one. She couldn't remember the name of the dance but liked it. For one, she couldn't get too mixed up.

They danced past the Featherstones. Agnes wore her usual sour expression and rolled her eyes when she saw them. Dora hoped Billy didn't notice.

When the music ended, he gave her a bow and grinned. "That was fun! Now I'm gonna dance with my ma!" He was off like a shot and Dora hoped he found Mrs. Watson available. She was still seated at the piano.

"May I have this dance?"

She stilled at Phileas' voice, then slowly turned to face

him. "Why yes, you may. Seeing as how my dance partner is now harassing the piano player for the next one."

They looked at the small group of musicians at one end of the dance area. Billy was tugging on his mother's arm, trying to get her away from the piano and onto the grass. She finally relented and let Billy take her into the crowd. "He's persistent, I'll give him that," Phileas said.

"He's having fun," she said. "And he's not a bad dancer."

"Oh?" He stepped closer. "Does this mean you'll be comparing my dancing skills to his?"

She smiled. "Of course."

Phileas laughed. "Then I can't wait to hear who the better dancer is." He took her hand and led her into the crowd.

Dora noticed folks were forming circles for a quadrille. Thank goodness she knew a few of those too. But did Phileas? "You're familiar with our country dances?"

"I've been to a few back home. They're not that different from these. However, I apologize in advance if I step on your feet."

"I feel it only fair to give you the same warning. I'm sorry in advance."

He turned to her. "Now that that's settled, let's prepare ourselves."

The music started again and before she knew it, they were going in a circle with others, breaking off into smaller groups, switching directions, then doing it all over again. Phileas didn't miss a step, but she did. She hadn't danced in a long time and her knowledge was limited. She only knew three dances and though this was one of them, she kept tripping over her own feet.

"Do be careful," Phileas advised on more than one occasion. Thankfully, he didn't complain and didn't make faces at her. She wished Captain Stanley was here. Now there was a man that could dance. He knew all sorts of dances and could have given her a few pointers before this evening. But alas, he was still in Bozeman. She hoped he was able to find a preacher and bring him back. Otherwise, how were her friends supposed to marry? Would they have to go to Virginia City and seek out a preacher there?

Her heart sank as she realized all her friends were getting hitched. The only one left was Alma, and she wasn't good friends with her like she was with Letty, Cassie, and Jean. There was also Etta Whitehead the blacksmith, but she hardly knew her at all.

"Something wrong?" Phileas asked.

She looked at him, saw the concern in his eyes, and a small part of her melted. "No." Dora looked away. It was nice to see someone worry for her, even for such a small thing. Phileas didn't even know what was wrong, yet asked anyway. Did anyone else notice?

She watched the other townsfolk as they danced around them. They were happy, laughing, having a good time. Wallis and Jean danced with the circle of folks next to hers and didn't so much as look their way.

"You're doing fine," Phileas commented.

She looked at him again, met his gaze, and her heart skipped. She blinked the sensation away. "Thank you. I guess I'm getting it now."

He smiled as the music stopped and people clapped. "I think you always had it. But it's nice to use your skills now and then to keep them fresh."

Dora smiled back as they clapped then left the dance area. She could do with a cookie or four.

Chapter Three

Phileas watched Wallis and Jean across the breakfast table. She'd no doubt dine with them from now on, and he tried to imagine what he could do with her place. He was supposed to see it today, but frankly, couldn't imagine what he could add to what Wallis had already done. The place was so small, Jean could decorate it herself. She didn't need his input.

Besides, he already knew that if Wallis and Jean married and stayed in Apple Blossom, they'd probably take over Sarah Crawford's house. If Jean wound up going into business with Sarah, then she could rent her own place out. To whom, he had no idea. Unless Captain Stanley found more than a preacher in Bozeman to bring back to town. Hmm, what more did the town need at this point other than a doctor and preacher?

He'd have to think about it.

Phileas studied the table. The bright blue gingham

tablecloth, the cheerful sunflowers in a dark blue vase, and the colorful bowls of sliced peaches, plums and blueberries next to a big tureen full of oatmeal were perfect. The table was indeed enchanting, and he couldn't for a moment imagine what he could contribute to it. Dora was a good decorator in her own right. She just needed some direction.

He had to admit the hotel and town were charming. Both were small but had all the amenities one could want given their size and, with the help of himself and his brothers, were getting small pockets decorated. If he had his way, he'd paint the entire hotel and some of the other buildings in town. Let's see, he could use colors with warm golds, deep reds and oranges, bright blues and deep greens...

He gazed at the front lobby. The furniture was handmade and appeared to be sturdy. He thought it was all very inviting and appreciated the attention to detail Dora's parents had paid to the place. But that was a long time ago. Now some walls needed painting and re-wallpapering. The windows had curtains that needed to be replaced. At least there were plenty of knickknacks and artwork to add to the inviting feel. He could imagine himself in this place, enjoying a good book and a glass of lemonade on a long summer evening.

As he watched Wallis and Jean chat in the kitchen, the thought struck him that if he ever married and had a home, he'd want it to be like this. Unfortunately, when he returned to England, that would not be the case.

Mother ruled the house and its servants. It was decorated the way she wanted it. And though the place was richly furnished, it wasn't homey. Not like this.

He had to admit, the small town of Apple Blossom was the perfect place to start a life. It might not have all the amenities of a big city but had a friendliness and charm he'd not seen anywhere else. Just think if he really made the town into something special. If he could do that, he'd be tempted to stay himself.

He watched Wallis and Jean again. The thought of them staying warmed his heart. He'd be sad to go, but if he took care of things here and ran the estate well, he might come back someday.

Phileas sighed. He needed to concentrate on the here and now. He'd have to put his ideas on paper and decide which part of the hotel to tackle first. With so little time left to him, this wasn't going to be easy.

As he finished his coffee, he had the fleeting thought he could bring Jean and Wallis back to England with him... he gave himself a shake. That was ridiculous. As was the thought he could make the hotel and Apple Blossom more than just a charming little town.

He had to be content with decorating the hotel with a few of the things he had in mind. Chintz fabric and bright, cheerful prints, colorful pillows. All the small touches that would remind him of his family and his home. It was a start. But ... he wasn't staying, so why was he thinking of fixing the place that way?

He sighed and drained his coffee cup. "I'm ready when you are, brother."

Wallis smiled. "Good. We'll take a look, then you can astound us with your advice."

"I'm sure you've done an admirable job already. I heard about some purchases you made at Alma's store."

"From Alma?" Jean asked with a smile.

"Who else? She even told me about the vase you bought."

Jean giggled. "Wallis. He bought everything, the dear." She rested her head on his shoulder. "I don't know what I would have done without his help and advice this last week. Now the library is open and filling with books, and my place is getting a new life."

Phileas smiled. He shouldn't ask, he already knew the answer. Still, he was curious. Maybe Wallis wanted to return to England. Not that it mattered. Phileas was the older of the two, so if Sterling, Irving, and Conrad didn't go back, he was next in line to take over the estate and title. "And your plans include the two of you residing there after you're wed?"

Wallis and Jean exchanged a smile. "We thought to speak to Sarah about buying her place," Wallis said.

Phileas nodded. It was just as he'd thought. "You've discussed this already?"

"Last night." Jean looked at Wallis. "You'll tell them?"

Sterling smiled. "You're staying."

They nodded and smiled.

"Well, that settles it, then. The sooner we finish Sarah's place the better." Phileas looked apologetically at Dora. "I'll start on the hotel as soon as I'm able."

"You'll start on it now," Sterling said.

"Yes," Conrad added. "We can finish Sarah's house. Now that Oliver isn't as, shall we say, pungent, he can help."

Oliver, sitting at another table, sank a little in his chair. "Then I might as well join you at your table for dinner."

"By all means," Irving said with a grin. "Just don't get sprayed again."

Oliver shuddered and got back to eating.

Phileas smiled. It seemed he wasn't the only one attached to the place. Everyone was staying, and that was a good thing, he supposed. Now his brothers had a fresh start, a real home. But for him, things would be different, and he tried not to think about it.

He made a mental note to make sure the hotel was the most beautiful place in town. He wanted it to be filled with warmth, love, and happiness. The thought gave him a thrill and a new purpose. He'd always known he'd return to England, but now he looked forward to putting his ideas into action and creating something beautiful for his brothers, their future wives, and the whole town of Apple Blossom. Even though he'd have to return home, he'd know he'd left behind a masterpiece to be enjoyed for years to come.

Would his parents care? No. Would they ever want to

see it? Definitely not. But Sterling, Conrad, Irving and Wallis deserved no less. He'd give them something to remember him by.

"Phileas," Oliver said behind him.

He jumped. "Where did you come from?" Good grief, he didn't see him leave his chair.

"Do you mind if I go with you to Jean's place?"

Phileas glanced around, noticed Sterling and Irving had left the table, then ran his hand over his face. "Why not?" He left his chair.

The two of them walked out of the hotel together, and as they did, Phileas had the strong feeling this place was home. He'd miss it dearly when he returned to England. Apple Blossom and the hotel were special places, and he'd keep them close in his heart.

He took a deep breath as they walked to Jean's. He'd miss them all, especially Wallis and Jean. But his time in Apple Blossom had been wonderful, and he'd never forget the friendships he'd made. He only hoped he could do enough to help the town grow and thrive.

Phileas took another breath and was understanding why Sterling was having such a struggle, but it was obvious he'd decided to stay. Whether or not he himself fell in love, leaving Apple Blossom would not be easy when the time came.

Dora cleaned up the breakfast dishes, took them into the kitchen and placed them in the sink. She noticed Phileas watching Wallis and Jean earlier, and wondered what was going through his head. Not that it was hard to guess. He was probably counting the days until he left for England. That gave him maybe a week to work on the hotel. Selfish as it sounded, she wanted to get as much out of him as she could in that time. The hotel was her livelihood, and if it looked good, people would want to stay there.

She prepared to do the dishes and looked around the hotel kitchen. It didn't look bad but could do with some sprucing up. The kitchen sink was clean, the dishes would soon be washed and dried, the floor swept and the counter clear except for a single bowl of bread dough that she intended to punch down soon. The way Phileas ate last night, maybe she should have made two loaves. Well, if she needed to, she would. In the meantime, she busied herself with the dishes.

Afterward, she studied the kitchen floor. She should mop it. Her eyes drifted to the curtains in the windows next. She needed new ones. And she had to admit, a new set of china was in order as well. Other than that, this room should be the least of Phileas' worries. Then again...

Her gaze turned to the kitchen table. She needed to rid it of its clutter. Dora reached for a stack of papers and saw one was a notebook, the pages filled with Phileas' handwriting and drawings. She smiled. He planned to use his last week in Apple Blossom to make the hotel into something special. Had he sketched any ideas in it? She didn't want to pry, and gently placed the notebook back in its place amongst the stack of papers.

Dora wanted to thank him, but with the way he'd been acting lately, was afraid he might not receive it well. He'd made great sacrifices and she knew it wasn't easy, so she quietly prayed he would have a safe journey back home. Just as soon as he finished the hotel.

Okay, so Phileas and his brothers had made an enormous impact while in Apple Blossom. His presence would be sorely missed when he was gone. With his help, the town was changing, and it would only get better when he finished the hotel.

Dora washed her hands in the left over dish water, dried her hands and offered silent thanks for his hard work and dedication. Things wouldn't be the same without him, but she knew Apple Blossom and its people would always remember him. And if she were lucky, he'd return one day. He had to. His brothers were staying behind. She smiled at the thought then covered the bread dough with the dish towel.

That done she took up her usual post behind the hotel's front counter. Not that there would be bevies of guests stampeding through her door, but she had high hopes of housing the new town doctor for two nights while he got settled in. Now that Jean was almost done with the library, maybe the two of them could look at the doctor's house and do some cleaning.

Speaking of cleaning, she forgot to dust. With a sigh,

she returned to the kitchen and got back to work. She dusted the hutch and hummed a tune. Usually, Jean helped her clean up the kitchen, but today she'd left with Wallis and Phileas and gone straight to her place. No wonder she was muddled.

Her thoughts still on Phileas, she polished the furniture in the lobby and even measured some curtains in the lobby windows. All that remained were Phileas' personal touches. All of Apple Blossom would be waiting for that.

When Dora returned to the counter, she sat and stared at the hotel doors. If she could will guests to come through them, she would. Having the six Darlings here reminded her of how much she enjoyed serving guests, cooking their meals and becoming engrossed in conversations with them. Hotel guests were her view into the rest of the world, and she feared that after Phileas and Oliver left, life would go back to being routine. Even though four of their brothers would stay behind, they'd be wrapped up in their new brides and building lives for themselves in Apple Blossom.

She pulled a book from beneath the counter and started to read. Maybe she should pay a visit to the new town library, but as far she knew, Jean wasn't there today.

She was about to run upstairs to her room and grab a different book, when Alma entered the hotel. "Dora!" she gushed. "Captain Stanley's back!"

She set her book down. "He is? Did he bring a preacher?"

"No, but he has someone with him. He's handsome too."

Dora raised an eyebrow but said nothing. Instead, she calmly slid off her stool, went around the counter and out the hotel doors. She could see the captain's wagon parked in front of the saloon, Captain Stanley barking orders. Sterling and Letty looked like they were helping him unload. And, as Alma said, there was a man with him. He was tall and had black hair. Even from this distance she could see he was handsome. But who was he?

Alma grabbed her hand. "Come on, let's go introduce ourselves."

"Alma, that's not how it's done." Dora pulled her hand away and held it to her chest. "For crying out loud, calm yourself."

"You think it's the new doctor?" Alma spun to the hotel doors and closed them. "I suppose if he is, then Agnes will be along soon."

"You're right. Maybe we should say hello before she commandeers him and tells him how horrible we all are."

Alma gasped. "She wouldn't, would she?"

Dora made a face. "Of course she would. It's Agnes." She started up the boardwalk.

Alma followed. "If he is the new doctor, has anyone cleaned the old doctor's house yet?"

"Not yet."

"I'll help," Alma offered.

"Thanks, we'll need it." Dora slowly approached the captain's wagon.

Captain Stanley caught sight of her and smiled. "Dora, come meet Mr. Hawthorne."

The dark-haired man approached from the other side of the wagon. He was as tall as Sterling, but with much darker hair and dark green eyes. "How do you do?" he said.

Her eyebrows shot up at the sound of his voice. It was Heaven.

"Hello," Alma said shyly.

"Begging your pardon, Mr. Hawthorne," Captain Stanley said. "But may I introduce Dora Jones? She's the innkeeper in our fine town."

Mr. Hawthorne chuckled. "I am familiar with the word hotel. Just because I'm from the East Coast doesn't mean I use our Eastern idioms in the West." He smiled at Dora. "Once again, how do you do?"

She tried to tear her gaze away, but it wasn't happening. This couldn't be Agnes's nephew, could it? "Very well, thank you," she finally said.

"And this," Captain Stanley motioned to Alma, "is Miss Kirk. She owns the general store." His smile broadened. "Alma?"

Alma stared wide-eyed at the gentleman. "Yes?"

The captain glanced between them. "I managed to convince Mr. Hawthorne to reside in Apple Blossom. After all, our town will be growing, and he could grow right along with it. Isn't that right, Mr. Hawthorne?"

The newcomer smiled and nodded, looking a little nervous. He stuck his hands in his pockets, took them out, then put them in again.

It didn't matter to Alma. She smiled, eyes bright, then asked, "So, other than Captain Stanley's kind words about our town, why move to Apple Blossom?"

Mr. Hawthorne shrugged. "Well, from what I can see, the town needs what I have to offer. He told me all about you, by the way."

If Alma's eyebrows could shoot up any higher, they'd reach the moon. "He did?"

He nodded and motioned toward the general store across the street. "He told me all about that too."

Alma's face went pink. "Oh, goodness, Captain, I hope you didn't exaggerate."

"I did nothing of the kind," he said with a frown. "I was realistic in my assessment of your store."

Her face fell. "What?"

"Face it, Alma, you don't have room to carry everything this town needs. So, I convinced Mr. Hawthorne to come."

Dora noticed Alma's expression had gone from exuberant joy (with a hint of "could this be a man for me?") to staring at Mr. Hawthorne like he was the family of skunks that sprayed poor Oliver. She turned her horrified expression to the captain, but all he could offer was a simple shrug.

Dora did the same. What could she do about it?

Except... "Mr. Hawthorne, what kind of business are you in?"

He smiled proudly. "I'm here to open a hardware store."

Alma gasped. "A what?!"

"You heard him," Captain Stanley said. "And it's a fine thing."

Alma glanced at her store and back. "No, it's not. I think it's horrible!"

Dora opened her mouth to speak, but Alma was already marching across the street to the general store. "Oh, dear. That didn't go over well."

Sterling and Letty returned to the wagon after taking a load of goods into the saloon. "What's the matter with her?" Sterling asked.

Dora sighed. "Mr. Hawthorne is here to open a hardware store."

Letty gasped. "A what?" She ran across the street to catch up with Alma.

Poor Mr. Hawthorne stared after them, mouth agape. "What did I say?"

Chapter Four

It didn't take long for news of Mr. Hawthorne's arrival to spread through town. Just as Dora had hoped, he would reside in the hotel until he could arrange for more permanent accommodations. There was an empty building next to the old dressmaker's shop, and another beyond that. The latter was larger, and she wondered if Mr. Hawthorne would buy it. He was well dressed and might have a bit of money.

Dora looked at the guest register. "Aaron J. Hawthorne." She glanced at the stairs. Whatever interest Alma might have had in the gentleman was gone. She'd hightailed it back to her store fast enough to leave a cloud of dust behind. Letty still hadn't come back—she must still be consoling Alma.

Dora shook her head at the thought, then sat on her stool. She fished her book from beneath the counter and tried to read. But with all the excitement, she couldn't concentrate. The contrast between Alma's own excitement over the newcomer, followed by her horrified expression at hearing about his store, wouldn't leave her head.

Now that she thought about it, Alma was the smart one. She wasn't about to let herself fall in love with one of the Darlings. They were too risky, and though Alma dreamed of traveling one day, she still wasn't going to allow herself to fall in love with someone that might leave Apple Blossom and never come back. But a handsome local was another story. However, considering Mr. Hawthorne had probably fallen into the "mortal enemy" category, Alma wasn't going to spend any more time than she had to with him. He was a threat to her livelihood.

Dora sighed and returned her book to its place beneath the counter. Maybe she should go across the street to Jean's place and see how things were shaping up there. She figured Phileas and the others would have returned by now. Jean's home was so small, there wasn't much to be done.

She left her perch, crossed the lobby to the hotel doors and looked out the windows. Jean was carrying a can of paint around to the front of the building. "So that's what they're doing. Finishing the painting."

She sighed and stepped outside. Phileas appeared with a ladder and set it against the right side of the structure. Jean handed him the paint and a brush, and up he went.

They were using yellow paint, and once finished, the funeral parlor would be a happy looking little building. Dora smiled and wondered if it was Wallis' idea to use that color. Phileas had spoken little about Jean's place until recently. His mind was on the hotel, and she hoped it stayed there until he could get to it. If, he ever got to it, that is. Mr. Hawthorne might lure Phileas away with refurbishing whatever building he set up shop in.

She went back inside. Would Phileas consider staying longer so he could do both? Dora sat on her stool and pondered the possibilities. She so wanted the hotel worked on and wasn't sure she could stand any more delays. It would just be her luck to run out of time and watch Phileas and Oliver ride out of town, her hotel untouched.

She slipped onto her stool, her heart in her throat. "It wouldn't be fair."

"What was that?"

She looked at the stairs. Mr. Hawthorne was coming down.

When he reached the last step, he smiled at her. "I'm off to inspect some buildings. I understand the large one next to the bank is already taken?"

"Yes, one of the Darlings purchased it." She took a moment to study him. He had changed clothes, but these were just as nice as the ones he'd had on earlier. "Mr. Featherstone owns the bank and the vacant buildings. You'll want to speak to him."

"Thank you." He tipped his hat and strolled out the

door.

She looked at the general store across the street. Poor Alma was in a dither over the newcomer. But it could only help her in the long run. If she no longer carried as many tools, she'd have room for other items. If another dressmaker didn't come to town, she could add more fabric and sewing notions to her store.

She continued to stare out the window, an odd emptiness growing in the pit of her stomach. She realized how Jean must have felt before Wallis declared his love for her. Their friends were getting married and would start lives with their new husbands. Soon they would have children and who knew how often they'd all get together? Dora might see very little of Letty, Cassie, and Jean.

At least the latter caught the attention of one of the Darlings. But there would be no such attention for her. She heard what Phileas told Oliver. He didn't plan on falling in love. His heart was in England and that was the end of it.

She sighed again and went into the kitchen to put her bread in the oven. She'd make some sandwiches for lunch, then think up something for dinner. Now that the hotel had another guest, she was full. If Agnes' nephew showed up before Mr. Hawthorne got himself some permanent accommodations, she'd have to turn him away—something that hadn't happened in the history of the hotel.

Once her bread was baking, she made herself a cup of

tea and sat at the kitchen table. Her mind kept wandering to thoughts of Phileas putting up new wallpaper, painting, hanging portraits and mopping floors with her. They were silly thoughts, but they were there all the same. He said he wouldn't be falling in love, and she'd better make darn sure she didn't either.

She took a shuddering breath. "Oh, goodness. I wouldn't, would I?" Who was to say? Love struck the Darling men and her friends like lightning. What if she was helping Phileas wallpaper one afternoon, gazed at him beside her, and became lost in love's web? He would leave, and she'd have nothing but a broken heart to remember him by. Unrequited love was the worst kind, and she didn't want to go through that.

When lunch time rolled around, Wallis, Jean, Phileas and Oliver showed up and sat at the usual table in the dining room. Irving, Sterling, and Conrad must be having lunch with their intendeds. Mr. Hawthorne joined them, however, and that brought some interesting conversation. "You're British," he told the men, stating the obvious. "How many of you are there?"

"Six of us," Phileas said. "We're on holiday, touring the wilds of America. But as you can see, we've been waylaid here."

"Waylaid?" Dora said. "You make it sound as if you're stuck here."

Phileas looked sheepish. "I didn't mean to." He smiled and surveyed the dining room. "I must say, I'm looking forward to working on this place."

Her heart warmed at his words. "I'm glad to hear it."

"So, are you some sort of decorator?" Mr. Hawthorne asked.

"After a fashion," Phileas said. "I have a knack for it." He winked at Dora and picked up his sandwich.

"Hmm," Mr. Hawthorne mused. "I looked at the small building next to what was once a dressmaker's shop. I looked at the dressmaker's shop too, but neither would suit my needs. Too small."

"So, you'll take the larger building?" Dora asked.

"Yes, I'm going to rent it from Mr. Featherstone, set up shop and see what happens." He took a generous bite of his sandwich and smiled.

Jean glanced at Dora and back. "And you're putting in what kind of business?"

Dora reached for her iced tea. She knew Jean had to have heard all about Mr. Hawthorne by now, even if she hadn't run into Alma. Letty would have told her before she went home to her ranch. Sterling would be with her and the two were probably discussing the addition of Mr. Hawthorne's hardware store at this very moment.

"I'll be selling building materials, tools, fencing, all sorts of hardware."

"Well, I think it's a jolly good idea," Wallis said.

Jean put on a cheerful smile. "Yes, Alma could use the extra room in her store."

Dora nodded. "That's what I thought, but convincing Alma might not be so easy."

Mr. Hawthorne put down his sandwich. "I'm not a

threat to her business. If anything, she'll bring business to me, and I'll do the same for her." He glanced nervously around the table.

"That remains to be seen," Oliver said. "But I can see how it would also free up space at the livery stable and feed store."

"Making room for more inventory is always a good thing." Mr. Hawthorne looked around the table again. "Um, how long do you think before Miss Kirk speaks to me?"

Jean almost spewed iced tea before she laughed. "That also remains to be seen."

Dora looked sympathetic. "I'm afraid you won't make a friend of Alma any time soon."

He nodded. "Good to know. But I'll do my best not to upset her further."

Dora looked at Phileas. He was staring back. What could he be thinking?

Phileas studied Aaron Hawthorne as Oliver began asking questions. The man looked to be Wallis' age and had been educated in Boston. He hailed from there as well and came west to Montana Territory to start a business and perhaps study law. Though Phileas had no idea where he would do that here. There were no universities or other places of higher learning for hundreds of miles. Did his parents want him to become a lawyer, or was he doing it for himself? He'd ask but didn't want to learn anymore about the young man than he had to.

He caught Dora staring at him a few times, and the thought that Mr. Hawthorne might court her stung. It shouldn't, but there was nothing he could do about it either. Things were what they were, and he had to focus on what lay before him. The hotel, then home.

He sighed and fixed his eyes on the table. He could imagine the look on Mother's face now. She'd be furious his brothers didn't return with him. She'd blame him, then turn her wrath on poor Oliver. Hopefully, he'd come away unscathed. Then the questions would fly like arrows, and she'd demand to know everything they could tell her about the young women that stole her sons away. She'd claim they were after the estate and the family money, but that wasn't the case. None of the women knew about their true identity until after each of his brothers proposed.

"And so, my brother Artemis finished school and ran off to Africa. No one's seen him since. Though we get letters now and then..."

Phileas looked up at the sound of Mr. Hawthorne's voice, saw the way Jean and Dora stared at him with wide eyes, and tried not to roll his.

"How fascinating," Dora said. "And he's your older brother?"

"By two years." He smiled at Phileas. "About your age, I'd say."

Phileas smiled back. "Is that so? Africa? Cape Town, I presume?"

"Artemis travels all over. He's a hunter you see and does some business on the side. My parents have investments there ..."

"What sort of investments?" Dora wondered.

Phileas cringed. Was she becoming interested in Mr. Hawthorne, or his brother?

"That's my family's business, but it's nothing too exciting." He smiled and took another bite of his sandwich. He was almost through and wouldn't have a reason to stop talking after a few more bites.

Phileas thought he'd ask a few of his own questions, but what was the point? He didn't have time to get to know the man and didn't care to. Unless...

He gave Dora a sidelong glance. Would this Hawthorne be a good match for her? Hmmm, if so, maybe he should take the time to get to know him better. He didn't want her taking interest in a man who didn't know a whit about running a business. Great Scott, he might try to stick his nose into her business and run the hotel. What if he ran it into the ground? Did she own the building or did the bank? He never asked. He made a quick mental note, then listened as Oliver continued to question Mr. Hawthorne about growing up in Boston.

He comes from money, Phileas concluded. His eyes darted to Dora and back. But he still wasn't sure if he should steer her in the man's direction or warn her about him.

Phileas blushed, knowing his thoughts were no doubt written all over his face. He turned away abruptly, hoping no one noticed. He hadn't been this confused around a woman since he first met Sarah, Irving's intended. At first he didn't know if she was interested in Irving or not, but at least after a little time passed, he knew the outcome before it unfolded. It was obvious Irving was interested in the widow and her children. With this, only time would tell. For now, he'd wait and see, and help Dora in any way he could if things got out of hand.

He tried not to roll his eyes. He shouldn't be thinking of Aaron Hawthorne as some cad come to rob the residents of Apple Blossom. From the sounds of it, he'd succumbed to the lure of the West like so many others, including himself, Oliver, and the rest of their brothers.

The meal over, he left with Wallis and Oliver to finish painting the funeral parlor while Jean offered to help Dora. Mr. Hawthorne disappeared upstairs to his room and Phileas didn't miss the bounce in his step. He seemed pleased with himself and probably was.

He crossed the street with his brothers and looked toward the saloon. "Do you think Captain Stanley is an excellent judge of character?"

Oliver slapped him on the back. "Don't tell me you don't trust Hawthorne?"

"I didn't say that."

"No," Wallis said. "But you were thinking it, weren't

you?"

Phileas smiled. "Perhaps."

Oliver laughed. "If you're that suspicious, then speak to the captain. He wouldn't have brought him if he thought this Hawthorne was up to no good."

Phileas had to give Oliver credit. He might be the youngest, but he had a knack for seeing the good in people. He was a better judge of character than Phileas any day.

Shrugging off his suspicions, Phileas stood before the funeral parlor. He had a job to do, and worrying about Dora's future was not part of it. Besides, he didn't know Hawthorne well enough to form an opinion yet, but realized he wanted to know more about him.

He glanced once again at the saloon and wondered why Hawthorne was in Apple Blossom. He had the feeling the young man was more than he was letting on. He'd keep an eye on him and try to adjust his opinion in the time he had left. After all, Dora would need a good man by her side, especially when the hotel was complete. He just hoped Aaron Hawthorne had it in him to be that man. If he did, then Phileas could leave Apple Blossom knowing she would be well taken care of.

Oliver went to the half-empty can of paint they'd left by the ladder. "What's on your mind?"

Phileas sighed. "I'm not sure."

"About what?"

"I bet I know," Wallis said. "He doesn't want anyone interrupting his work on the hotel. Hawthorne might."

Phileas picked up the brush he'd placed in a bucket of water earlier. "That's not it. I worry he might try to horn in on Dora's business, or worse, they might…" He snapped his mouth shut. So what if she ended up marrying the man? He glanced over his shoulder at the hotel. "What am I supposed to do? I've only so much time to help her and can't afford any more interruptions."

Oliver shrugged. "Only one thing you can do. Keep an eye on him."

Wallis nodded. "Keep your friends close and your enemies closer. You should watch Hawthorne and, if you're worried, take steps to protect Dora and the hotel. He may be a gentleman, but don't take any chances."

Phileas gaped at them. He couldn't believe they'd been thinking the same thing. Then again, they'd all grown fond of Apple Blossom and its residents. It was only natural they'd be protective. "Agreed," he finally said. He headed for the ladder, took the can of paint from Oliver and started up. There was a small patch he didn't get to before lunch and wanted it done.

When they finished painting the building, he'd see what other paint Alma had on hand for the hotel. He didn't have time to order any more. He had his eye on a few colors and wondered how much he'd have to have his eye on Aaron Hawthorne. Would he be a good fit for Dora, or a disaster for her and the town?

Time would tell, but what would it be able to tell Phileas in what little time he had?

Chapter Five

Dora sat on the bench in front of the hotel for a while after lunch and watched Phileas, Oliver and Wallis work. Jean had disappeared inside, and she didn't want to bother her. So she headed across the street to Alma's store to see how she was faring. Besides, she needed a few things and might as well take care of both at once. She knew this could take a while.

When she entered, Alma stood behind the counter, dusting shelves like a mad woman. "Land sakes, what's the rush?" Dora asked. "The dust isn't going anywhere."

Alma jumped with a yelp and turned around. "Oh, it's you." She faced the shelves again and resumed her furious dusting.

"You make me sound as if I'm of no importance." Dora leaned against the counter.

Alma turned around and tossed the duster onto it. "I'm sorry. It's just that *man*!"

Dora sighed. This might take longer than she thought. "Give him a chance. Everyone thinks Mr. Hawthorne's venture will be good for your store."

She pointed toward the vacant buildings up the street. "He's opening a hardware store. How does that help me?"

Dora studied the array of goods surrounding them. "For one, it would be nice if you carried more ready-made clothes. You could put another display over where the shovels and rakes are, expand your fruit and vegetable display and..." She thought a moment. "You could order some furniture."

Alma's jaw dropped. "Furniture?"

She walked across the storefront to where several wheelbarrows were placed. "What about a dining room table and chairs? You could decorate it with tablecloths and sets of dishes. You've always wanted a hutch in here." She walked to the bins of nails. "It would look great in this spot." She turned to Alma. "When you think about it, who does most of the shopping in this town?"

Alma cracked a smile. "The women."

"Yes." Dora shook a finger at her. "Let the men go to the hardware store for their tools and things, then the women can have this place. You can carry more of the things we want to buy."

Alma slowly nodded, but still glared at the doors leading outside. "Do you think Etta knows? If he sells fencing supplies that takes business away from her."

"Then she'll have more room for hay, grain, and

other things a feed store should carry. She's not a lumberyard."

Alma sat in a chair by the large potbellied stove. "I suppose you're right, but that still doesn't mean I have to like him."

"No one said you did." Dora sat in the only other chair. There was a small table with a checkerboard on it, but the only people that ever played were gone now. Her father being one of them. He used to love coming here to play with Mr. Kirk. She pushed the thought aside. "Promise you'll be civil to him? He's the first newcomer here since the Darlings, and with any luck, he'll stay."

"Who says I want him to?" Alma crossed her arms and frowned.

Dora sighed. "What's wrong?"

Alma stared at the wide floorboards. Dora followed her gaze. They were nicked and scratched from use. She used to enjoy sitting on the floor next to her father as he played checkers with Alma's pa.

"I don't know," Alma whispered. "I guess I'm a little put out that nothing's going to get done here."

Dora brushed a lock of hair from her eyes. Was Alma crying? "Hey, it's all right. Sterling, Conrad, Wallis and Irving will still be here to help you."

"Yes, but..." Alma licked her lower lip, then bit it. "They're not Phileas." She looked at Dora. "You're the lucky one. He wants to work on the hotel something awful." She glanced around the store. "But this place? Not so much."

"I thought you were fine with the store."

"Yes. It's not like it needs a lot of fixing as far as floorboards and squeaky door hinges. But Phileas works magic on anything he touches. Have you seen Cassie's place? And what about Letty's? They're both beautiful. I haven't seen what he's done to Sarah Crawford's house, but I'll bet it looks good."

Dora nodded. "Maybe in a couple of days I'll stroll down the road and take a look."

"I'll go with you." Alma left her chair and went to the table covered with ribbons, hairbrushes, and combs. "I need a bigger table."

"I think the captain might have one you could use." Dora stood. "I could ask him now if you'd like."

Alma smiled, then wrinkled her nose. "Am I being childish?"

Dora fought a smile and made a face instead. "Maybe a little."

Alma sighed. "I can't help it. This place has been all anyone in Apple Blossom ever needed. I feel... threatened."

Dora's heart went out to her. "Oh, Alma, don't think that way." She pulled her into a hug. "Mr. Hawthorne isn't here to take your business away. You're still going to be the only general store in town."

She nodded. "I know, but I can't help it." She stepped out of Dora's embrace. "I don't know what's wrong with me." She hugged herself as she went behind the counter. "Did you need anything?"

Dora pulled a small list from her apron pocket. "Here." She put it on the counter.

Alma took it and began gathering what Dora needed. There was only so much anyone could do for her right now. Alma would have to figure out why Mr. Hawthorne made her feel the way he did.

As she waited, Dora thought of what Alma said about Phileas. Was she lucky to have him work on the hotel? Very. And Alma was right. If he took the time to do some rearranging in the store, he might make it into something special. After all, anything the Darlings touched became that way. She couldn't wait to see what would happen with the bakery Sarah and Jean wanted to start. Too bad Phileas and Oliver wouldn't be here to see it. By then they would be gone, and she feared a part of her would go with them.

When Alma finished, Dora paid her, then went across the street. There was no sign of Phileas and the others. There was also no sign of the ladder or paint cans and buckets. They must have finished. Were they back at the hotel?

She entered but didn't see anyone. The men were probably upstairs getting cleaned up. They might have also gone to Sarah's house to work.

Dora went to the kitchen to fix a cup of tea and see to dinner. She could make a stew easily enough. She had everything she needed. A good thing too, she didn't want to go back to Alma's.

She put the kettle on and set out a teapot, cup and saucer on the worktable.

"You read my mind."

She gasped and jumped back. "Phileas, I didn't hear you come in."

He smiled. "It's because I oiled the hinges on the swinging door. You don't want them squeaking when you come in and out of here, do you?"

She stared at the door leading to the dining room. She hadn't realized he'd done it. "When?"

He shrugged. "A few days ago." He went to the hutch and helped himself to a cup and saucer. "Are there any cookies?"

She smiled. "There are always cookies."

He set his cup and saucer next to hers, then went to fetch the cookie jar. "You'll need to make more. Oliver's coming downstairs in a few moments. Though I'm not sure if he'll stop in here for a cup."

She did her best not to look at him. He was a wonderful decorator and so much more. He was handsome, intelligent, kind, sophisticated. Of the six Darling brothers, he was the most gentlemanly. He walked differently from the rest, almost as if he were royalty. Sterling walked like he was born to lead, but he didn't have the regal bearing Phileas did. She was fascinated because even though the six were brothers; they were all so different.

They talked about their lunch with Mr. Hawthorne while the water heated, then made their tea. Oliver still hadn't come down, so Phileas wrapped some cookies in a napkin for him and put them in his pocket.

"You're not going to save any for Wallis?"

He laughed. "Jean was making some sort of dessert while we were finishing up her place. He's probably stuffing himself with it as we speak." He took a generous bite of cookie and smiled.

Dora nodded. One thing about the Darlings, they loved their sweets. She wrapped a few cookies in a napkin for him then handed Phileas the bundle.

"For me?"

She nodded. "Otherwise, you'll steal Oliver's."

He laughed. "You're so right!"

Dora smiled in satisfaction. "I do try."

He downed the rest of his tea, checked his cookie-filled pockets, then gave her a parting nod. "I'll see you at dinner."

Dora smiled again, her heart in her throat. "Until then."

He left, making a show of swinging the kitchen door back and forth, a hand to his ear, then disappeared.

She stared at the door as it still swung. "Goodness me. I'm going to miss that man."

Phileas and Oliver watched Wallis and Sterling put the finishing touches on Sarah's bedroom floor. "There, at last we're done," Sterling said. "Now all we have to do is clean a few things up and Sarah and the children can move back in."

Oliver sniffed the air. "The smell isn't too bad. I wonder if the skunks are still around."

"If they are," Phileas said, "then we need to ensure they don't take up residence again."

The brothers looked at one another. "A dog, perhaps?" Wallis suggested.

Sterling made a face. "I don't know how Irving will feel about that."

"Come now," Phileas said. "Irving loves dogs."

"True, but they'll be living in town once they're married."

All heads turned to Wallis. He shrugged. "I love dogs too."

"Good," Sterling said. "The skunks will hate one."

Wallis sighed. "I do hope Jean likes dogs."

The rest laughed as Sterling and Wallis began gathering tools. Phileas wanted to polish the floor for Sarah and make it shine. He could always stay behind and take care of it before the furniture was moved back in.

"You have that look," Oliver said.

He smiled. "I need to do something with this floor. Would you mind helping me?"

"Not at all. How long will it take?"

"Not long with the two of us working." Phileas strode from one end of the room to the other. "All we need to do is sweep things up in here, then give the floor a good once over."

Oliver crossed his arms and leaned against the door-jamb. "I never took you as one to enjoy hard work."

"This isn't work, brother. This is beautification. There's a difference." Phileas went to the window and looked at the curtains. They were new, like the rest of the curtains in the house. Irving took care of the cost and he hoped he didn't regret all the money he spent only to have Sarah and the children live somewhere else.

They got to work as Wallis and Sterling headed back to town. They'd return when they could. Phileas wasn't in a big hurry and didn't mind walking back in the dark. The sooner they got the house ready, the sooner Sarah and the children could enjoy the fruits of their labor.

By the time they got done, the sun was setting, and Phileas began thinking about the hotel. "I'm going to paint my masterpiece tomorrow. I'll announce it at dinner."

"By the time we get back, dinner will be over." Oliver grinned at him. "So what are you going to do first?"

"The lobby, of course. It must make a good first impression. I want new curtains, wallpaper, the counter must be polished and waxed, the shelving as well, the chairs and sofa should be re-upholstered..."

"Whoa!" Oliver laughed. "You don't have time to do all that. Not if we're to leave as planned."

Phileas stopped in the middle of the road. "Yes, about that." His hands went to his hips. "What if we postponed our return?"

Oliver's jaw dropped. "What?"

"We could send word to Mother and Father. It wouldn't be unusual for us to want to stay a little longer. There's so much to see and do here. Don't you want to see San Francisco and not just hurry through it to get to our ship?"

"Yes, but... what will Mother say?"

"Oh, she'll rant and rave to be sure, then take it out on the servants, Father, the gardener, the neighbors, the vicar, and probably the entire village given half the chance." He closed the distance between them and put his hands on Oliver's shoulders. "But we're talking about a masterpiece. I want to leave Apple Blossom with something extra special. Something to rival that hotel in..." he cocked his head. "What's that town called again?"

"What town?"

"You know, the one the duke of Stantham told us about."

Oliver scratched his head. "Um, I can't remember."

He shrugged. "No matter, suffice to say, I want it to rival that fancy hotel in Oregon. That town is no bigger than Apple Blossom and its hotel built by that Van Cleet fellow."

Oliver nodded in remembrance. "Oh, yes, The Van Cleet Hotel in Clear Creek."

"Yes, that's it! Jolly good." Phileas slapped him on the back, and they continued down the road.

By the time they reached the hotel, dessert had been served and only Dora, Sarah and Irving were at the table. "Where have you two been?" Dora asked.

"Did you keep something warm for us?" Oliver asked.

"Lucky for you I did. The stew is on the stove. Have a seat and I'll bring you each a bowl." She headed for the kitchen's swinging door. When she reached it, she looked Phileas in the eyes, swung it back and forth a few times, then went into the kitchen wearing a smile.

"What was that about?" Oliver asked.

Phileas laughed. "She didn't notice I'd oiled the hinges until I told her."

Wallis laughed. "She's making fun of it?"

"Not at all. I think it's her way of saying thank you."

"She'll be telling you more than that once you're done with this place," Sarah said. "By the way, why are you so late? What happened at my place?"

"Nothing," he said. "I wanted to make sure your floor was at its best."

She blushed and smiled. "You're too kind, Phileas. Thank you." She looked at Oliver. "And you."

Oliver ran his hand through his hair, then put it to his chest. "For being wounded in the line of fire?"

Sarah laughed. "Something like that. Flint thinks you're a hero."

"For putting my life in danger?" Oliver laughed. "Nothing anyone else wouldn't have done."

"Speak for yourself," Phileas quipped. "I'd have climbed a tree to escape those horrible beasts."

Everyone laughed as Dora returned with two bowls

of stew. She set them on the table. "I'll be back with some bread."

The men watched her disappear again as Sarah smiled. "She talked about the hotel throughout dinner." She sighed and looked at Phileas. "Dora's worried you won't be able to finish what you start. Will you?"

He exchanged a look with Oliver. "I've already thought of that. How fast could I get a message to England?"

Dora gasped. She stood at the kitchen door. It swung inward and back, smacking her in the rump. She ignored it and came to the table. "What was that?" She set the plate of bread down. "You want to get a message to England?"

He turned to her and smiled. "I'll need to discuss it with Sterling and the others, but yes. I want to give this place the time it deserves."

Her hands flew to her mouth. "You'd do that for me?"

He gave her a warm smile. "Of course. Your hotel deserves as much attention as Sarah's home or anyone else's we've worked on." He looked around the dining room. "And let's face it, this is much bigger."

Without warning, she threw her arms around his neck. "Oh, Phileas, thank you!"

He smiled, noticed how much he enjoyed the closeness of her, and brought her hands down. "There, there, you didn't think I'd short you?"

She wiped a tear from her eye. "I didn't know what

to think." She smiled at Sarah. "I'm sure your place looks wonderful. I can't wait to see it."

"Come see it sometime. Could Jean watch the hotel for a couple of hours?"

"I'm sure she won't mind." Dora turned to him. "Oh, but do you need me?"

"Tomorrow I'll confirm the list I originally made and adjust it accordingly."

"Based on what?" she asked.

"Time remaining. I'm not sure what that will be."

"Oh, it's your parents, isn't it," she said. "You have to get back and then give them the news of Sterling, Conrad, Irving and Wallis." She pulled out a chair and sat. "Will they be horribly upset?"

Oliver laughed weakly. "You have no idea."

"But won't they be happy for them?" she asked.

Sarah looked at them and shook her head. They knew better than to tell Dora who and what they really were. It might put too much pressure on her, and she'd insist they leave as planned. But that would mean only part of the hotel would be done, and Phileas didn't want to do that to her. She'd waited long enough for her turn, and he was determined to give it to her.

"We'll talk about it tomorrow." Phileas took his seat. Oliver followed suit and soon the two were wolfing down their dinner. Sarah excused herself to go find Irving and the children, who were paying a visit to Captain Stanley. As soon as she was gone, Dora slumped in her chair.

"There now," Phileas said softly. "You'll be all right and so will the hotel. I'll see to it."

"But I don't want it to burden you..."

"Nonsense. Besides, once I figure out exactly what needs to be done in what order, I'll enlist the help of my brothers. This place will take priority, and we'll get as much done as we can before Oliver and I leave."

She stared at him a moment and he wondered what she was thinking. She looked...sad. Did that mean she didn't want him to go?

Phileas turned back to his food. He didn't have time to think about that. He had too much work to do. Besides, he had no business falling in love with anyone from Apple Blossom. He had his duty, and it wasn't here.

Chapter Six

D ora didn't know why she was upset. She'd been fine with Phileas working on Letty, Cassie, Sarah and Jean's places. That is until she thought about the time factor. And her time was running out. But if Phileas extended his time in Apple Blossom, then she'd not only get her hotel finished, she would have more time with him. She already felt like she'd been sharing him.

When the Darlings first started working on some houses, she thought it was nice and kind and generous of them to do so. But she also kept getting shoved to the back of the line and found she was tired of it. She'd be left with nothing if this kept up. If Phileas and Oliver stayed a few extra weeks, that would solve everything. Maybe they'd even still be here when the town got a new preacher. Still, who knew when that would be?

She took the dishes to the kitchen once the men were

done eating, gave them some pie, then retreated to the kitchen to start the evening chores.

"Need any help?"

She smiled at the sound of Phileas' voice and continued to pour hot water into the wash basin. "Yes, thank you."

He joined her at the sink. "I'll wash, you dry?"

"Fine." She felt herself blush and had no idea why. She and Phileas had done the dishes lots of times since he'd been here. But now that his leaving was so close, she could feel her heart pinch every time she was with him. For Heaven's sake, it's not as if she was sweet on him or anything.

They started the dishes and she thought of what to say to start a conversation. Thankfully, he did it for her. "Reds or blues?"

"What?"

He gave her a side-long glance. "Red or blue wallpaper. Though green is nice too."

"Oh. Well, I like green."

"Then green you shall have. I thought of red, but I think green is better considering you're surrounded by orchards."

She smiled. "I never would've thought of that."

"So we make the hotel an extension of the natural beauty around it." He looked at her, his eyes roaming her face for a moment, then looked away. "And upstairs? Alma still has a decent selection of wallpaper. Enough to do several rooms in the same pattern, then several more in another. I had her order some soon after we arrived and stepped into our roles as repairmen." He winked.

Dora's heart skipped. "You have no idea how much all the work you've done means to us and the rest of the town. It's been nice."

"But we've not done anything for you yet."

She laughed. "Yes, you have. You're guests of the hotel. You've been providing me with income. Now Mr. Hawthorne is here along with Sarah and the children."

"But the Crawfords aren't paying—you're letting them stay for free, despite protests from Irving."

"I know, but having all these people here makes it feel... well, like a home."

He stopped washing the plate in his hand. "What do you mean?"

She drew in a breath. "It was rare the hotel was full. In fact, I think it only happened once, and that was a large group passing through years ago. They were on their way to Virginia City for a relative's funeral and stumbled upon Apple Blossom much like you did."

"Yes, but could they wallpaper?"

She laughed. "I have no idea. But I remember how happy Pa was to take care of them."

"Hospitality is an art, Dora." He winked again. "Your father sounds like he was a natural born host. So are you."

She blushed again. "I don't know about that."

"It's true, you've taken wonderful care of us since we arrived. Thank you."

Her blush deepened as she took the plate from him and dried it. "What else is on your list?"

"Paint, of course, curtains, doors, windows, all should be checked for cracks and things."

She nodded. He was right – she hadn't thought of that. "Is your room drafty?"

"No, but Irving's could be looked at. The window doesn't quite shut all the way and rain has damaged the sill. I might have to replace it."

"Oh, dear. And the window?"

He looked sheepish. "That depends on whether I accidentally break it while fixing the sill."

Dora laughed as Irving, Sarah and her children entered the kitchen. "Is there any pie left?" Flint asked.

"Even if there was," Sarah said, "you can't have any. It's your bedtime."

"Aw, Ma," he whined. "I'm still hungry."

"Then have some leftover stew." She went to the pot. "Can he?"

Dora smiled at them. "Of course, help yourselves." She took the bowl Phileas handed her and dried it. She watched Sarah dish up some stew for Flint, then spoon what remained into a large bowl and place it in the icebox. There was enough for lunch tomorrow if she made some biscuits and a salad to go with it.

She smiled at Phileas as Sarah, Irving and the children sat at the kitchen table. "Running this hotel is like having house guests all the time."

"You consider this your house?" he asked softly.

"Yes. I know it's silly, but that's what it's always felt like to me."

He smiled. "I understand. I suppose if one loves to entertain, then it's the perfect job."

She gave him a shy smile. "Do you like to entertain?"

To her surprise, he blushed. "Well, I've hosted an affair or two. They're fun."

"What sort of affairs?"

"Well, let me see. Picnics. Dances, a couple of musicales, though my mother did have a heavy hand on most. She wouldn't have it any other way."

"Is she meddlesome?"

He stopped washing and looked at her.

"Oh," she gasped. "I didn't mean to offend you..."

"On the contrary, sometimes I think you know her."

She shook her head. "She sounds like a busy woman who brooks no argument when she wants something done."

He laughed. "That's her."

Dora tried not to smile. "She reminds me of Agnes."

"Oh," he said and cringed. "Wouldn't that be a meeting of the minds?"

"What's that?" Irving said from the table.

Phileas grinned. "Mother and Agnes meeting face to face."

Irving stopped whatever sort of conversation he was having with Sarah, eyes rounded to saucers. "Bite your tongue, man."

Phileas chuckled and turned back to the dishes. "I think we're about done here."

Dora tried not to smile again. Only this time, she'd been admiring his bare forearms and the way his muscles moved as he washed another dish. "Yes. Thank you for helping."

He handed her the last bowl, then eyed Flint's. "Is he about done?"

Flint chewed and grinned at him.

"He is." Sarah took Flint's bowl and handed it to Phileas. "Thank you, Dora. Dinner was wonderful. I'll help you with it tomorrow."

"Thank you." She nodded at Sarah and the others as they left the kitchen, then started putting dishes away.

Phileas leaned against the sink and watched her. "So this is your big house and you're doing what any hostess would do after a large dinner party. Cleaning up."

"I like to think so." She put a stack of bowls in the hutch's cupboard, then opened the drawer where she kept the silverware. "And you helped me. Just as you do every night."

He joined her at the hutch. "And after we put everything away, we'd go for a stroll up and down Main Street."

She put the last of the silverware in the drawer then turned to face him. "Yes."

He smiled as he looked into her eyes. "Then what are we waiting for?"

She smiled back. "I don't know."

He offered her his arm. "Shall we take our stroll?"

Dora wiped her hands on her apron, took it off, then looped her arm through his. The last thing she did was toss her apron onto the worktable as they left the kitchen. They were acting out a dream, but her heart still reacted as if this was real and Phileas would never leave. If only it were true.

As they walked, Dora's heart pounded in her chest. This was a game, nothing more. A few moments of make-believe that Phileas was obliging her. It was silly and wonderful. It also made her realize she was lonely. She'd not been on a man's arm before, other than her father's. Phileas didn't so much as bat an eye at the contact and she wondered if he could tell how nervous she was. Would her breathing give her away, or that she was beginning to sweat?

Good grief, what was wrong with her? It wasn't as if she hadn't been spending part of every day with the man since he arrived in town. But now... well, things had changed. He was leaving, and she was hit with what she'd be missing. If he managed to stay longer, how much worse would it be when he left?

"You're quiet," he commented as they reached the livery stable.

"I'm sorry, I was thinking about all the wonderful things you're going to be doing to the hotel. I can't wait."

"You're going to help me, of course?"

"Of course." She took a shuddering breath.

"Are you all right?" He took off his jacket and put it around her shoulders. "There."

The jacket was warm and smelled like soap, apples, and him. The weight of it gave Dora a heady sensation, and she didn't want to take it off, although the evening was warm. She hardly needed it. "Thank you."

"Have you thought of a chandelier?"

She blinked. "What? Oh, dear, I could never afford..."

"In the dining room. It would add a touch of elegance." He smiled at her. "And reflect the hotel's hostess."

A chill went up her spine, and she did her best to breathe normally. She was acutely aware of how close he was, despite them no longer walking arm in arm. "A chandelier can do that?"

"The entire hotel will." He stopped and turned to her. "Dora, if you want me to do this right, you'll have to trust me."

"I do, but..."

He gave her a warm smile. "But what?"

"Will you have time?"

He grinned. "I ordered the chandelier the moment I saw it in Alma's catalogue."

She sucked in a breath. "You did? When was that?"

"A few days after we started working on Letty's place.

It should be here any time now. Along with a few other things."

Her hand flew to her mouth. "Oh, Phileas. I can't afford such an extravagance."

He took her arm and pulled her a step closer. "I took care of it. I hope you don't mind."

She shook her head in disbelief. Was he serious? "But... I don't know when I can pay you back. I have some money set aside for the hotel. Enough for the wall-paper and to fix a few windows..."

"But you want the place to shine, don't you?"

He had her there. "Yes."

"Then let me work my magic, Dora. You won't regret it."

How could she let him spend his own money on her like this? "I can't charge your brothers and you anymore for your rooms. Not when you're going to be doing all this work for me."

"Nonsense, of course we'll pay for our stay. Besides, they're not that expensive." He winked at her and let go of her arm.

Her eyes cut to it and back. She could still feel the warmth of his hand and closed her eyes a moment, committing it to memory.

They strolled to the other end of the street, then to the sheriff's office. It was dark here, quiet, the sky bright with stars. It was also romantic, but all she could do was dream about romance. Phileas had no interest in her, especially not when he was returning to England. But look what happened to his brothers. Would the same thing happen to him? To her? She was, after all, the other part of the equation in this.

But what if there was another part? What if by some odd occurrence, Phileas took notice of Alma or Etta? What then?

Her heart sank, and she fought the chill racing up her spine. Oh dear, she wasn't jealous, was she? Land sakes, she was only thinking of it. There was nothing supporting what was in her mind's eye.

"Dora?"

She shook herself. "Sorry, there's so much to think about."

"I agree, which is why I want to go over my old list with you tomorrow. You'll have time, won't you?"

"I don't see why not." She cleared her throat. She had no idea what to make for breakfast or dinner and needed to take care of that before she did anything else. But the lure of Phileas' offer was sinking into her bones and if she wasn't careful, she'd spend all morning with him and get nothing done.

"Right after breakfast?" he prompted.

"Sure, that would be nice." She smiled, unable to help herself. Spending more time with Phileas at this point might not be such a good idea, but now was her chance to have him at her disposal. She needed to take advantage of that.

When they returned to the hotel, he opened the door for her and they went inside. "I should head up," he said.

"Unless there's anything else you'd like me to do for you?"

She shook her head and looked into his eyes. "No, nothing." She swallowed hard, her throat suddenly dry. Oh, heavens.

He gazed at her now. "Then I shall retire. Until tomorrow."

She nodded, unable to speak. What was happening?

He nodded back and slowly headed for the staircase. "By tomorrow afternoon, we'll know what to do and I'll enlist my brothers to help. We'll have this place done in no time and you'll have the gem of Montana Territory."

She laughed. "It's hardly a gem, but I'll settle for a nice shiny coin."

"Nonsense, by the time I'm through, this hotel will be all anyone between Virginia City and Bozeman talks about."

She smiled as he winked once again then ascended the stairs.

Dora let out the breath she was holding. How much more wonderful could a man be?

Chapter Seven

Dora closed her eyes for a moment, opened them, then went down the hall to her living quarters. It wasn't until she reached her door that she realized she was still wearing Phileas' jacket. She turned toward the lobby, smiled, then went inside her little parlor. After she closed the door, she pulled the jacket tight around her shoulders then went to the window. She'd give him his jacket in the morning.

Until then, she'd figure out a way to keep her heart well-guarded. She'd taken his presence for granted up to now and kept herself from daydreaming. Now her dreams might get the best of her.

When morning came, she spied the jacket draped over the back of a chair and smiled. She'd stared at it before falling asleep and wondered if spending so much time with Phileas was going to do more harm than good. She was beginning to understand what happened to

Letty and the others when the Darlings worked on their places—she'd have to be extra careful not to fall under the same spell. These men were handsome, with wonderful accents, manners and no shortage of kindness and charm. What woman wouldn't fall in love with one of them?

She went through her usual morning routine, dressed then went to start breakfast. No one was up. She liked the early morning hours, alone in the kitchen with a cup of coffee and the smell of the cookstove. There was a nip in the air, but the kitchen was the warmest room in the hotel.

She sat at the table, sipped her coffee, and ticked off a mental list of chores she had to perform that morning. Somewhere in there she had to fit Phileas. Who knew how long it would take, but that was okay. She was getting her turn. Problem was, would she come away with a nicer hotel and her heart intact, or broken?

Oliver and Sterling were the first to come into the kitchen for coffee. Next came Irving and Flint, who went straight to the table and waited for the oatmeal she was preparing. Wallis came next, followed by Sarah and her daughter Lacey. The little girl clutched her newest doll to her chest and eyed the pot of oatmeal on the stove.

Dora looked at the kitchen door. "Where's Phileas?"

Sterling smiled. "Don't worry, he'll be along."

Mr. Hawthorne entered, went straight to the stove and eyed the coffee pot. It had become apparent over the last two mornings that the man was slow to wake and didn't put together a coherent sentence until after he'd had a few cups. He also hadn't noticed the hotel's homey atmosphere and that no one waited in the dining room to be served their coffee. Instead, they got it themselves, then went into the dining room to await breakfast or sipped their coffee in the kitchen for a time.

Dora poured him a cup, then steered him toward the table. She was like a mother with a big family. The only thing missing was a husband.

Irving and Conrad entered and went straight to the table. "Good morning," Conrad greeted. "Are we eating in here this morning?"

Dora's eyes widened. "Oh, dear, I forgot to set the tables in the dining room!"

"It's all right," Sarah said. "We don't mind."

Dora stared at the others in shock. She'd been so busy thinking about Phileas, she didn't do one of her main chores. "I'm sorry, everyone."

"It's Phileas," Oliver said. "He has her muddled already."

"Does he?" Sterling asked with concern. "Don't let him do anything you don't want him to. He'll treat this building like he owns it and who knows what it will turn out like?"

She smiled, hand to her chest. She was probably red as a cherry. "I trust him. I guess I'm excited."

"As well you should be," Phileas announced as he entered. "Because today, I begin my masterpiece!"

Some of his brothers rolled their eyes and groaned.

79

Dora smiled. It was all in good fun, but she couldn't help wondering if Phileas' love of art and beauty made them cringe occasionally. After all, what did farmers usually know of such things?

Everyone went into the dining room and settled down to eat, interrupted now and then by Flint, who was already trying to worm his way into helping Phileas with his enormous task of sprucing up the hotel. Billy hadn't approached him yet about lending a hand, and Flint was trying to position himself as Phileas' second-in-command. Hmm, where did that put her? She giggled at the thought and added some honey to her oatmeal.

When the meal was over and the dishes done, she pointed at the kitchen table. "Okay, Mr. Darling," she said. "Let's get down to business."

Flint, who'd been getting ushered out the kitchen door by his mother after he raided the cookie jar, stopped dead in his tracks. "Wait!" He held onto either side of the door frame. "I want to help."

Sarah heaved a sigh. "You need to come to the house with me to help with your room."

"But Ma," Flint whined. "We're going to live in the big building by the bank."

"Not yet we aren't." She tried to pry his hands from the door frame.

Phileas laughed. "Flint, I'll need your help, but not today."

The boy let go and spun around to face him. "What are you doing today?"

Phileas smiled. "Prioritizing." He gave Dora a wink. "Right?"

"Oh, yes," she said. "We can't start any work until we know what needs the most help."

Flint's face screwed up for a moment before he nodded. "Okay. But as soon as you know, tell me. And don't tell Billy!" He darted out the door to the hall. His sister Lacey skipped after him.

Sarah sighed and shook her head. "He's eager to make money. I'm sorry if he's pestering you."

"Not at all," Phileas said. "The boy is learning how to earn a wage. That's a good thing. Perhaps one day he and Billy will have a business together."

Sarah smiled, then slipped out the door and down the hall.

"I envy her sometimes," Dora said without thinking. She stiffened then glanced at Phileas.

He was looking right at her. "Why?"

She swallowed. "Isn't it obvious?"

He turned to the door. "The children?"

She nodded. Sometimes when she watched Sarah with Flint and Lacey, she had a pang of envy. She wanted children one day, but first she'd have to get one of those elusive things called a husband. How, she had no idea. Men were scarce in Apple Blossom up until the Darlings arrived, and the two left weren't sticking around. Mr. Hawthorne popped into her head, but so far all he was interested in was his hardware store.

"Now, let us sit and discuss our plan of action." Phileas went to the table and pulled out a chair for her.

Dora smiled, sat, then waited for him to take his own seat across from her. He had paper and pen ready to go. "The lobby should be our first priority."

"I agree. Strip the wallpaper. Fix the windows and doors if they need it, then put the new wallpaper up. Alma has had a few things come in over the last week and has been holding them for me."

Her stomach did a little flip. That he'd gone to so much trouble for her warmed her heart. But was he really doing it for her, or for himself? If he were a painter, would he paint her portrait because it brought him pleasure and a sense of pride, or because she asked him to? Were they the same thing? She didn't think so.

"Let's take a stroll across the street and fetch the wallpaper and a few other things."

"All right." She stood. "What can Flint do to help?"

He grinned. "I've thought of that too. He can work on the counter, polishing and waxing. If he uses your stool, he can reach well enough."

She smiled. "You've thought of everything, haven't you?"

"I do try." He headed for the door to the hall. "Can you get away for a few moments?"

"Of course. We're just going across the street. If anyone rides up to the hotel, we'll be the first to see them."

"You're quite right. Besides, if we don't spot them, Alma will."

She smiled. He knew as well as she did Alma was the eyes and ears of Apple Blossom. Besides Agnes, of course.

They went to the general store and Alma was more than happy to bring out the wallpaper, brushes, and a few knickknacks Phileas had picked out for the lobby.

Dora ran her hand over a roll of wallpaper. "This will look wonderful." She gave him a sly look. "You knew I'd pick green."

"Well, I admit I looked at the black and white Alma already had on hand, but the green fit the hotel better."

She smiled, caught Alma's conspiratorial wink, then tried to visualize the finished product. She wished Pa were still alive to see this. Phileas was right—this was going to turn the hotel into a masterpiece.

"Wait until you see the chandelier," Alma gushed.

"For the dining room?" Dora glanced at Phileas. "It's here already?"

"Any day now."

She smiled, her heart climbing into her throat. Such a wonderful man. If only he were staying. "Well, how nice." She cleared her throat and turned away, a tear in her eye. If she wasn't careful, she'd be in love with him before the week was out. It was fine when he worked on Letty, Cassie, Sarah and Jean's places. Now that it was her turn, she was overwhelmed at his kindness and that of his brothers.

His hand rested on her shoulder. "Are you quite all right?" His voice was gentle, with a hint of concern.

"Of course. Just... well, you're going to spoil me."

"Of course." He leaned a little closer. "It wouldn't be any fun otherwise."

Dora gasped and thought she might die. Goodness! Did he have to stand so close?

Thankfully, he stepped back and gathered up the rolls of wallpaper. "We'll take these now, Alma. Dora dear, could you bring the brushes?"

She stared at him, her mind clinging to the simple endearment. "Of course." She took the brushes from the counter and followed him to the double doors leading outside. "Wait, don't you have to pay for this? Or do I need to?"

He stopped and gave her a warm smile. "It's all taken care of." He winked then pushed open one door with a free hand.

They crossed the street to the hotel and went inside. Agnes was outside the bank, watching them. Dora hoped she didn't head their way and start asking questions. Nothing could ruin her day quicker than a run-in with Agnes. That went for most folks in Apple Blossom.

Phileas excused himself to fetch some tools from his room, then hurried up the stairs. In the meantime, Dora put the large kettle on the stove to heat. They'd need hot water to dissolve the glue of the existing wallpaper before putting up the new.

It wasn't long before Phileas joined her. "Well, this

will be fun. How long do you think it will be before Flint gives his mother the slip and joins us?"

Dora laughed as she watched the kettle. She didn't dare look at him. He was in his element and couldn't wait to get started. Seeing him happy made her happy, and that couldn't be good. She didn't want to walk the path of love. It would be a stupid thing to do. *Don't look at him, don't look at him, don't look at him.*

"You know, staring at the kettle won't make the water heat any faster."

She turned to him. Oh, blast. His eyes met hers and part of her melted on the spot. He was forbidden fruit and she dare not take a bite. "Oh, I wasn't watching it..."

"Weren't you?"

Dora shook her head, turned around and stared at the kettle again. Okay, she *was* staring. But better at the kettle than him.

🐚

Phileas watched Dora out of the corner of his eye. She was happy, and he noticed the way she smiled every time she pulled some wallpaper off the wall. Funny how such a mundane task could make her eyes brighter than before, and her countenance one of pure joy. Had he put that smile on her face?

He pulled off another piece of paper. He could work faster than she could, as he had a longer reach. They brushed on hot water, waited, brushed on some more,

KIT MORGAN

then began stripping the paper from the walls over two hours ago. Dora showed no sign of stopping. "You should take a break," he suggested. "You're, um, sweating."

She stopped, looked at him, then wiped her brow with the back of her hand. "Oh. I'm sorry, I had no idea."

He smiled. "You're working hard, but it's not going to get done any faster if you push this hard. You'll be sore tomorrow."

She smiled weakly. "Sorry. I didn't think about that. I want to help you every day."

"Then let's take a break. Tea?" He climbed off the ladder he'd been using and headed for the kitchen. She quickly followed.

At the stove she checked the kettle. "There's just enough for a pot." She went to a hutch on the other side of the kitchen where she kept the tea and some other things for cooking. "I'll have a pot ready in a moment."

He fetched the cookie jar and put it on the table. "Are you tired? Do you need to go lay down for a while?"

She spun to him. "Of course not." She spooned tea into the teapot then got the kettle from the stove. "What gave you that idea?"

He sighed. Her face was red from her exertions, and she was still sweating. "Oh, I don't know..."

She looked at him and made a face. "I'm just excited, that's all. It's my turn and I want to take advantage of the time we have. For all I know, you could be gone in a matter of days."

He studied her a moment. The worry etched into her features was hard to miss. "You needn't fret. I'll finish even if it means Oliver and I stay on a few extra days."

She looked at him. "Days?"

"Dora," he said and left the table. "I'll stay as long as I have to." He stood on the other side of the worktable and looked into her eyes. My, but they were nice, even if they were full of worry. "I'll take care of this place as if it were my own."

She swallowed hard. "I...have no doubt you will." She finished pouring water into the teapot then looked at him again. "Even if it means staying on weeks?"

He looked at the pot, then her. Dora Jones was spunky, well read, pretty. Of course, he'd stay a few extra weeks if he had to. Who wouldn't want to spend extra time with her? But was that wise? He'd told himself he wouldn't fall in love and had no intention to. But here was a woman that had caught his eye almost from the first day he arrived in Apple Blossom.

But was it really her he was enamored with, or her hotel? He did love a good project and he'd never get to do this in England. He'd be laughed at. What gentleman of his standing would lower himself to work on a ramshackle hotel and make it into something special? He could only imagine what his mother would do.

"Is...something wrong?" she asked.

Phileas shook his head. "Nothing. I'll get the cream." He went to the icebox and brought the cream to the table, then fetched the sugar. If he didn't want to fall in love, then he'd better concentrate on the hotel and only the hotel. Oliver could help while his other brothers finished up with any other projects in town. One of which was Etta Whitehead's place. Good grief, he almost forgot about her! "Dora, tell me about where Etta lives."

She poured tea into their cups. "She has a room behind the blacksmith's shop."

He gaped at her. "What? That's it?"

She nodded. "It's a large room. Etta and her pa divided it with a rope and a few quilts. I thought you knew."

Phileas closed his eyes and shook his head. "No, I didn't. I'm not sure any of us did. Oliver looked at the livery stable and feed store as a whole. We didn't think about her living quarters." He went to the table. "But Oliver had to have seen them."

"He probably did," she agreed. "But I'm afraid where they sleep might not have looked like much."

He sat. "How big is the room?"

She shrugged. "Maybe about the size of this kitchen. There are a couple of cots, a small stove. The Whiteheads have lived there since they came to Apple Blossom about six years ago."

He stared at her. "Poor Etta. And now she's been trying to survive carrying on her father's work? But... she's so petite."

"That she is. But she's fiery. Always has been. And she has a way with animals. Horses love her."

He took the cup and saucer she offered. "That helps

when one works with them." He took a sip of tea, added some sugar, and took another sip.

"I know she's waiting her turn. It's another reason I worried about this place. I know you'll want to finish both before you leave."

He sat back and thought a moment. How was this going to go? They'd have to split into teams and work on both places. And if Etta didn't have a decent place to live in, what good would it do to clean up a room with nothing but a cot and a stove? "I'll have Oliver look at Etta's living quarters again. Then he can tell me what he thinks of it." He heaved a sigh. "I feel like we've overlooked Etta. I'm sorry."

She poured cream into her cup. "She's not one to complain."

"And that's why she's not said a word to any of us." He took a sip. "She's poor." It was a simple statement, but it made his heart pinch.

Dora stared at the table a moment. "She gets by. But yes, to most people, she's poor. There are only so many horses in this town to shoe."

"Can she do anything else?"

Dora shook her head. "As far as I know, the only thing her father taught her to do was shoe horses."

He nodded to himself. Come to think of it, was Etta at the dance? She must have been.

They finished their tea, had a few cookies, then returned to work. He noticed Dora didn't work so feverishly and smiled. She was finally taking it easy. Good. He still hoped she wasn't sore tomorrow. It would make the work all the harder.

They worked another hour and a half before Dora announced she needed to make lunch. Phileas followed her back to the kitchen to help.

"What are you doing?" she asked.

"What does it look like?" He went to the icebox and pulled out some ham she'd sliced up the day before, the leftover stew, she'd saved for dinner. "Helping."

She smiled. "Thank you." She fetched a loaf of bread and began slicing it for sandwiches. They made sandwiches for everyone and were just bringing everything to the table when his brothers began filing in. Even Conrad and Cassie showed up.

"You're actually eating with us, brother?" Phileas said.

"We thought we'd make sure the two of you weren't overdoing it on your first day." Conrad grinned then turned toward the lobby. "A good thing too. Great Scott, man, what a sight."

"Wait until you see the new wallpaper," Phileas preened. "It's going to be magnificent."

Sterling smiled. "You really have missed your calling." His smile faded. "But you know what Mother would say."

Phileas rolled his eyes. "Do I ever." He glanced at Dora and back. Mother would have a lot to say as it was, and he dreaded the day when he had to listen to all of it.

Chapter Eight

Dora watched Phileas throughout the meal. His concern for Etta's place was heartwarming, and she had a pang of guilt for thinking only of the hotel with Etta only an afterthought. She was ashamed but would help when the time came. Etta had money saved, but she didn't know how much. Could she afford to rent Jean's place from her? That way she'd have a newly decorated home.

But what if someone came along that wanted to be the new undertaker? Then what? No, there had to be a better solution, but what? Did Etta have enough saved to build a small cabin behind the blacksmith's shop? Dora would have to ask.

When the meal was through, Phileas helped her with the dishes then they got back to work. She was tired but wasn't about to say anything. She wanted this done now more than ever so Etta could have her turn.

"Don't work so fast," Phileas advised again. He stood next to her as he adjusted the ladder. "We don't have to strip all the paper off in one day."

She pulled off another piece. "I thought you wanted to stay on schedule."

He laughed. "I didn't have one. Not really."

"But you should. How else can you tell what you'll need?"

He smiled warmly. Could he tell how fearful she was of not finishing? "Shh," he whispered. "I'll finish in time, love. You needn't worry so."

Her jaw trembled slightly as she nodded. "Yes, of course." She got back to work and moved down the wall. The endearment made her heart melt. He was just trying to reassure her, that's all.

He cleared his throat and got back to work himself. Phileas probably used endearments all the time back in England. He probably called his mother "dear" now and then, and the neighbor's daughters or matrons. They would think nothing of it. But just now when he'd said it, well, it did something.

She didn't so much as blink at him as they worked, and she'd go across the room and start working over there if she had to. Then again, maybe she should take a quick break before having to start dinner. But part of her enjoyed working alongside him and she envisioned doing this every day. Well, maybe not stripping wallpaper, but working side by side.

He moved the ladder down to where she worked. "I think you've had enough."

She stopped, pulled at a long strip of paper and stared at him. "What?"

"Go on, take a rest, then do what it is you do."

She cocked her head. "Excuse me?"

He closed the distance between them and pulled the rest of the paper off. "Stop, Dora. You've done enough for the day." He looked into her eyes and smiled. "You're a hard worker."

She smiled back, nodded, then scooted past him and headed for the kitchen. The sooner she got away from him the better. So what if the lobby was in a shambles and the furniture in the middle of the room? She didn't even care that paper lay everywhere. She'd get to work cleaning it up in a moment. First, she wanted to take a break from Phileas before she forgot how to guard her heart.

Drat. Phileas entered the kitchen right behind her and she headed for the icebox. "What are you doing?" he asked.

She straightened, the cream in her hand. "Fixing another pot of tea. Would you like some?" She might as well ask since he was there.

He smiled. "Don't mind if I do. Then I'll clean up the lobby."

Her eyes darted to the kitchen door leading to the hall. "You don't think we'll get any random guests, do you?"

He laughed. "I don't think so. How often do you get guests?"

She set the cream on the table. "Rarely enough. Once you're gone, I don't know what I'll do." In more ways than one.

He smiled again. "It's nice to know I'm useful."

Her heart skipped. Did he say that because he meant it, or he thought she was using him and that was that? "Of course you are. All of you have been so helpful to us, Phileas." She closed the distance between them. "You have no idea what you've done."

He looked into her eyes. "I have some." He sat at the table. "Should we have another go at the cookies?"

"You'll spoil your dinner."

"Stripping wallpaper is hard work. If Oliver were here, you can bet he'd be in the cookie jar." He went to fetch it.

She fixed their tea and watched him munch a cookie. Was he going to eat more than one? He ate like a horse the night of the dance, and she'd concluded he ate when he was nervous. Was he nervous now?

She brought the cups and saucers to the table, poured their tea, then took a cookie for herself. "We'd better not eat anymore. I won't have time to make any tonight and have nothing else for dessert."

He smiled. "All the more reason for Jean and Sarah to open a bakery." He took a generous bite of cookie and smiled.

She sipped her tea slowly. A bakery would be nice,

but Apple Blossom was so small—could the money made from it support Jean and Sarah? After all, if Irving and Wallis stayed, what would they do to make money? The bakery couldn't support six people, could it? She watched Phileas reach for the cookie jar again. "What can Irving and Wallis do?"

He took one out, looking sheepish. "What's that?"

"Irving and Wallis, what can they do? Conrad is deputy and earns a wage, and Sterling can work Letty's farm with her. But what can Irving and Wallis do to make a living here?"

"Oh, that." Phileas dropped the cookie into the jar. "Well, Wallis can always help Jean with the undertaker business and the bakery."

"Yes, but what about Irving, Sarah and the children? Sarah can't be expected to run the bakery with Jean and do laundry."

"Oh, good heavens, no. Irving won't let her keep a laundry business. We all saw how hard she worked."

"Then what can he do?"

"Oh, um, perhaps you should ask him." He smiled. "I should clean up the lobby." He stood, drained his cup, then quickly left the kitchen.

Dora gaped at the door and stood. Why was he avoiding the question? If she were Sarah or Jean, she'd want to know.

She finished her tea then took out the leftover stew from last night. If everyone took a small portion, she could reheat it for dinner. She could make a salad, some biscuits, then they could have what was left of the cookies for dessert. She sighed. "It will have to do."

She looked at the kitchen door to the hall. Phileas was evasive earlier and it still bothered her. But it was a good question, and she wondered if Sarah and Jean had second thoughts about saying "I do."

Dora brushed the thought aside and tried to concentrate on gathering what she needed to make dinner. She'd have to go to Alma's for some fresh lettuce and was glad the local farms and some of the townsfolk sold the produce from their gardens to Alma so she could sell it to the rest of them. She had a small garden, but with this many people in the hotel, it wasn't enough. She'd exhausted what she had already.

Dora made a quick list then headed for the store. Phileas was nowhere to be seen as she passed through the lobby. He must have run upstairs for a moment. If he hadn't come down by the time she got back, she'd pick up the discarded wallpaper before tackling dinner. Maybe he was as worn out as she was and went upstairs to sit a few moments. Would he be offended she did what he said he would do?

Dora decided to let him clean up and she'd stay in the kitchen. It was becoming more and more obvious that the less time she spent with the man the better. Though that would be nearly impossible to do.

Phileas tried not to watch Dora over dinner. But every time she put food into her mouth, he thought of providing that food. The question was, how? He thought about what she asked earlier concerning his brothers and didn't want to tell her any more than he had to. Which made him think. Would Sterling or the others tell anyone else in town who and what they really were after he and Oliver were gone? Would they let the townspeople think they were mere farmers?

But they might become just that. If Father got upset enough and disowned the four, they would have to figure out something or starve.

He eyed Wallis across the table next to Jean. What could his brother do to support her? And Irving—he had three other mouths to feed, not just one.

He concentrated on his food and tried not to think about it. He'd make provision for them if he had to. Once Father was gone and he took over the title and estate, he could do what he wanted. Mother could gripe all *she* wanted, but he wouldn't let his brothers starve. Still, they'd have to do something. For one, he knew they couldn't sit idle for long, and two, their father could live a good long time.

Their lives would be much different here. This wasn't England. There were no hunting parties, no men's club, no operas or balls to attend. They were in a small town in the middle of nowhere and would have to eke out a living like everyone else.

He watched Sterling pop a small piece of tomato into

Letty's mouth. Love surrounded him, and he couldn't partake of it. What would become of the estate and title if he did? Oliver couldn't handle things and would need all of their help to do it. They'd have to make trips to England and too many of those trips would raise suspicion. They'd either have to tell everyone who and what they really were or..."Great Scott!"

"What?" Sterling asked with concern. "Phileas, what's the matter?"

"I... forgot to do something. Would you mind helping, brother?"

"Not at all." Sterling left his chair.

They excused themselves and went into the lobby. From there Phileas ushered his eldest brother outside. "I just thought of something."

"What?" Sterling looked up and down the street. "Should we be whispering?"

"Perhaps," he said in a low voice. "The new preacher, whomever he will be, is going to see your marriage licenses. All of them. And what name will be on those licenses?"

Sterling stared at him a moment. "Yes, I thought of that." He leaned against a post. "There's nothing to be done about it."

"But the whole town will know."

Sterling shrugged. "What will it matter by then?"

He shook his head. "We've been going by Darling to do what?"

Sterling stared at him a moment then came away

from the post. "Protect ourselves from being robbed, mostly."

Phileas glared at him.

Sterling's face fell. "Oh, I see what you're trying to say."

"Word will get out, and you know who will spread it?"

"Not Alma." Sterling ran a hand through his hair.

"Think of the *feather* you'll be putting in Agnes' social cap when she finds out she has nobility in her town. She'll spread the news from here to San Francisco. Then every bandit, kidnapper, and lowdown snake will come here thinking they can have a piece of all of you. Ransom, Sterling. They'll go after the women, possibly even Flint and Lacey."

Sterling raked his hair again. "I hadn't thought of that. I figured Apple Blossom's location was deterrent enough. No one passes through very often."

"No, because there's no reason to except as a stopover to Virginia City or Bozeman. But the sons of a viscount —now there's something to take a look at."

Sterling's jaw went slack. "Thank you, brother. You've given us something to think about. But there's no sense worrying about it until the new preacher gets here, then we'll speak with him."

"What can you do? Bribe the man to keep quiet?" Nervous, Phileas began to pace. "It's risky. And, as much as I hate to say it, wrong."

"We'll figure it out when it comes time." Sterling

took his arm. "Keep this to yourself for now. I don't want the others to worry."

He shrugged. "Love is blind."

"Indeed, it is." Sterling let go his arm and motioned him to the lobby doors. "We should return to dinner."

He nodded and followed Sterling inside. When dinner was through and dessert served, he went back to stealing glances at Dora between bites of cookie and sips of coffee. She looked tired – he'd have to make sure she didn't work so hard tomorrow. He knew she wanted to make sure he got everything done before he and Oliver left.

He composed a telegraph message in his head that would appease their mother. If he stayed a while longer, he'd have time to finish the hotel, work on Etta's place a little and Alma's store. The doctor would have arrived and maybe the new preacher as well. All would be in order, and he could leave knowing the town was in excellent hands. Then he and Oliver would go home and face the firing squad.

After dessert he offered to help Dora with the dishes. She didn't answer at first, and instead gathered up cups and saucers and scurried into the kitchen. He followed with the empty cookie plate. She was going to have to bake tomorrow. "I say," he said as he entered the kitchen. "But the cookie jar is empty. I'm afraid poor Ollie will have to pitch in tomorrow while you fill it."

She stood at the stove then turned around. "Oh, yes.

Fine." She took the huge cast-iron kettle and hefted it toward the back door.

"Here, let me do that." He took it from her, went outside and filled it at the pump. She must be so tired, she wasn't thinking. He always filled the kettle for the dishes. Why was she trying to do it?

When he returned, he put it on the stove. There was no sign of Dora. She must be in the dining room. He went through the swinging door and found her standing in the middle of the lobby. "What are you doing here?" He joined her. The walls were almost completely stripped. They had one to go and would take care of it tomorrow.

"We did this," she stated.

"Indeed. It was a lot of work but went fast with the two of us."

She looked away. "I'm sorry I won't be able to help you tomorrow."

"You have other things to take care of, Dora. A hotel to run. That's no small task."

She turned to him. "Thank you for helping me with it. You've been a dear."

His chest swelled. "I try. It's better than being an obnoxious oaf."

Dora giggled. "Yes, I would think so. I'm... going to miss your help."

Part of him wanted her to say she'd miss *him*, but that was ridiculous. Why would she say such a thing?

She looked him in the eyes. "I'm going to miss you too."

His heart stopped. Did he hear her right? "Well, I... suppose we've formed a friendship, haven't we?"

She nodded, her eyes still locked with his.

He gulped. "Oh, dear, the water. I should check it." He hurried into the kitchen.

Oliver was there staring into the empty cookie jar. "Gone," he said forlornly. "All gone."

"Never mind about the cookies," Phileas snapped. He glanced at the kitchen door. "Dora just said she'd miss me when I'm gone."

Oliver rolled his eyes. "They all will after what you've done."

Phileas shook his head. "You don't understand. She'll miss me. *Me!* I can't have that."

Oliver smiled. "What's the matter, afraid you'll fall in love?"

Phileas gave him a pointed look.

Oliver blanched. "What? But you can't!"

"I know!"

Oliver looked panicked. "What are you going to do?"

Phileas took him by the shoulders. "Ollie, you're going to have to help me *not* fall in love."

Chapter Nine

Dora tried not to think of Phileas that night but couldn't manage it. He kept popping into her head no matter what she tried. Finally, she sat up. "This is ridiculous!" She smacked her quilt for emphasis. Not that anyone was around to see the determined gleam in her eye, or the way she frowned. "I have to do something or I'm going to slip. But what?" She tried to think of a way to steer clear of Phileas without making it obvious. But if she did that, how could she help him finish the hotel? To get it done he was going to need all the help he could get.

When she finally got to sleep, she had part of a plan in her head. She just hoped it was still there when she woke up. Thank goodness, it was.

She dressed, went through her usual routine, then went downstairs to start breakfast. As usual, all was quiet, and she enjoyed a few moments of silence alone with her coffee. All the while, she tried not to imagine what it would be like to have Phileas by her side, the two of them making breakfast for hotel guests and serving them. It was a nice thought that made her chest warm, but it was not to be.

He was not only leaving but hadn't shown a single ounce of romantic interest in her the entire time he'd been in Apple Blossom. He was falling in love with the care and decorating of houses and beautifying the town. From mowing the orchards to painting Sarah Crawford's walls, he'd been enjoying himself. She couldn't put the same sort of smile on his face. And she'd seen a lot of smiles. As soon as he began working his magic on Letty's house, he'd return to the hotel every evening proud as a peacock.

Fine, he could decorate and preen over his accomplishments all the way back to England. She sighed. "If that doesn't deter me, I don't know what will." She left the table and got to work. She wanted to make flapjacks this morning and gathered what she needed.

Oliver entered the kitchen first and headed straight for the coffeepot. She was glad the Darlings felt comfortable enough to serve their own coffee and would miss having them around in the morning.

"Morning, Dora," he greeted. "What's for breakfast?" He reached for one of the cups she'd placed on the worktable.

"Flapjacks and bacon." She smiled at him then

cleared her throat. "Oliver, are you attracted to anyone in Apple Blossom?"

He almost dropped his cup. "Wh-what?"

She shrugged. "I only ask because I know you're going home soon, and I'd hate to see you with a broken heart or cause one."

He gawked at her. "I-I'm not in love with anyone, no."

"Then you're a smart man. What about Phileas?"

He gaped at her some more. "He isn't either."

Her chest tightened, but it was for the best. "Good. You should make sure he doesn't get attached to anyone or you'll be returning to England on your own." She gave him a pointed look. "Understand?"

He blinked a few times and nodded. Of the six, Oliver still had a touch of boyish charm and innocence. "Understood. No falling in love for Phileas."

She smiled. "Not that there's many to fall in love with." She sighed and turned back to her batter, giving the bowl a stir. "You'll keep an eye on him?"

He stared at her and nodded. "Yes."

"Good, that means you'll have to help him finish the hotel."

He nodded again. "I was planning to."

"Excellent." She smiled and got back to mixing. With Oliver helping, she wouldn't have to spend as much time with Phileas but would be close by in case he needed her help. With Oliver as a buffer between them, she was less likely to lose her heart.

By the time the rest of the Darlings filed into the kitchen (Mr. Hawthorne brought up the rear) Dora was feeling confident she wouldn't fall in love. All she had to do was get through the next week or however long Phileas and Oliver stayed on, then come out with her heart unscathed when they left. No mean feat if she had another day like yesterday. She couldn't afford that, but also couldn't stand the thought of not seeing Phileas. Yes, she'd grown attached, but was she in love? Of course not.

She ushered everyone into the dining room so she could start serving and noticed how quiet the Darlings were. Mr. Hawthorne was always quiet, but he wasn't awake and functioning yet. It wasn't like the brothers to..."Has something happened?" she heard herself ask.

Irving looked up from his coffee. "What makes you think so?"

"You all look..." She cocked her head. "... I don't know, like you're...stuck. Yes, that's a good word. Are you?"

Sterling looked around the table. "Why would you think that?"

She set the platter of flapjacks on the table. "You usually talk and tease each other. But I haven't heard a thing."

Sterling glanced at his brothers again. "Well, considering our time with Phileas and Oliver is becoming less and less, it's affecting us now."

Her heart sank at his words. She knew the feeling. "Yes, I understand. I'm sorry if I seem insensitive."

"Not at all," Conrad said. "We're going to miss them, that's all."

She smiled at Phileas, and before she could stop herself, "Me too," popped out. She spun on her heel and hurried into the kitchen. "Land sakes, what did you say that for?" She went to the stove to fetch the platter of bacon from the warming oven. "Now what will they think?"

After taking a moment to compose herself, she got the platter and stood before the door. She sighed, took in some air and sighed again. It did nothing for her racing heart. She hoped they didn't think she was sweet on Phileas. Would they say anything if they did?

She squared her shoulders and returned to the dining room. No one said a word as she entered and set the bacon on the table. Once seated, Phileas said the blessing and the meal began.

Dora noticed how quiet the others were and wondered who said what while she was in the kitchen. No matter, Phileas didn't have any feelings for her and probably said so right after she scurried to get the bacon.

Mr. Hawthorne looked around the table a few times as he took a few pieces. "So, when are you leaving?"

Irving buttered his flapjacks. "Phileas and Oliver are leaving. The rest of us are staying."

Mr. Hawthorne's eyes darted from one brother to the next. "And you're marrying?"

"That's right," Sterling said then took a bite of food.

Mr. Hawthorne nodded sagely. "And once married, you'll live here?"

All six Darlings looked at him.

"Of course they will," Dora said.

He shrugged. "I just thought, since they're marrying, they might take their wives home to England with them. Makes sense to me. Your livelihood is there, is it not?" He took a generous bite of bacon and continued to glance around the table.

"True," Wallis said. "But more than a few of us have an adventurous spirit and want to brave life in the Wild West." He smiled at his brothers, then began to eat.

Mr. Hawthorne laughed as he cut his flapjacks. "You can hardly call Apple Blossom wild. Not from what I've seen."

Everyone looked at him. As far as Dora knew, Mr. Hawthorne knew little about the posse that rode out that fateful day or the loss suffered when they never came back. Maybe it was time someone educated him. Even so, she could see his point. To the casual observer, Apple Blossom didn't have a lot to offer, and it was only a matter of time before others began to wonder how some of the Darlings were going to get along in the sleepy little town.

Phileas stripped off the rest of the wallpaper with his brothers looking on. "What form," Oliver quipped.

"Yes, one would think he's been doing this for years," Conrad added. He smiled at the rest who nodded their agreement.

"Have you been holding some secret, Phileas?" Irving asked.

He turned around, a long strip of paper in one hand. "Instead of commenting on the sidelines, why not help?"

"But you're so good at this," Wallis laughed. "We wouldn't want to deprive you of the pleasure."

Phileas rolled his eyes. "Dora was more help than any of you."

They looked at each other, then got to work. None of them wanted to be outworked by a woman.

He smiled. "Not only did she help me strip wallpaper yesterday, but still made lunch and dinner for the lot of us."

"She's a good woman," Sterling commented as he brushed hot water onto the last of the paper.

"Yes," Oliver said. "But whoever marries her is going to take on a lot of work."

"What? Nonsense," Phileas said. "Why, there's not that much to do other than some laundry, cleaning the rooms after guests leave, checking them in, some cooking. Face it, chaps, we're the most action this place has ever seen."

"But what if more people start coming to Apple Blossom?" Irving asked.

"He has a point," Wallis agreed. "Apple Blossom

could be made into something special, and it wouldn't take long to get the word out."

Phileas stopped what he was doing. "What?"

"The town should have a newspaper," Wallis said. "Or at the very least, a column in one of the larger papers. Perhaps one in Bozeman? It could be delivered by post."

Irving nodded and wagged a finger at the rest of them. "If the town were to have an actual festival, people could come from both Bozeman and Virginia City."

"Virginia City is much closer," Oliver said. "And has fewer people. If too many people came, there wouldn't be room enough at the hotel."

"They could camp just outside of town," Sterling suggested. "Letty and I were discussing this very thing last week."

Phileas looked at them. Since they were alone, he might as well bring up a few things. "Are you trying to figure out how to bring income to Apple Blossom?"

"Of course," Sterling said. "This town needs something to bring folks to it. If more people settled here, then businesses would move in. A cafe, a dressmaker, a real post office, a telegraph office. Maybe even a newspaper."

Phileas nodded then pulled off a few small pieces of wallpaper he'd missed. "It sounds like you're making the town into what you want it to be."

"What's wrong with that?" Conrad said. "After all, if we're going to live here, shouldn't we help the place out? The town doesn't even have a school."

"And who will build it?" Phileas asked. "Will Captain Stanley be the teacher and if not, then who? You?"

Irving glanced at the others and back. "Why not? If not me, then Wallis could just as easily do it."

Wallis made a face. "Right, you are, but... shouldn't the town hire one?"

"You were educated at Oxford," Sterling said. "We all were." He looked at Oliver. "You've just finished, but it still counts."

Oliver nodded and stuck his hands in his pockets.

Phileas sighed. It was one more reason Oliver wasn't prepared to take on the title and estate should something unexpected happen to their father sooner than later. Oliver had been away at school these last few years. The duty would fall to him and him alone. "Are you sure you're all staying?" he asked one last time.

Sterling looked at the others, then nodded. "Yes." He sighed, put a hand on Phileas' shoulder, then smiled. "We'll help you however we can."

Phileas sighed again. "Then you'd better make sure you're prepared for all that might entail. I have a feeling it will be more than having to deal with Mother and Father. You're going to have to deal with a lot of other things too." He looked at Sterling. He knew he'd spoken to a few of them about the dangers of revealing who they were in this wild country. But had he spoken with the rest?

"Wallis should become the schoolteacher," Oliver suggested.

Everyone looked at Wallis, who shrugged. "I can do it. Makes sense since Jean runs the library."

"And she'll be helping Sarah with the bakery," Sterling said. "Irving?"

"What?" He looked at Phileas. "I'll help wherever its needed."

"You need a job," Phileas said. "What can you do?"

Irving nodded. "You're talking about the little item Sterling brought up the other day, aren't you?"

"That's my guess."

Conrad rubbed the back of his neck a few times. "So, you're the one that brought it up first?"

Phileas nodded. "If you want to keep your brides safe, maybe it's better no one knows who you are."

Conrad laughed. "I'm the town deputy. What man with loads of money is going to stoop to such work?"

"You," the rest said at once.

Conrad blushed. "Well, all right. What other man would do such a thing? That goes for all of us. Yes, we're from England, but does anyone have to know the details of our lives before coming to Apple Blossom?"

"Not really," Sterling said. "But there are some in town who would blow things out of proportion should word get out before we want it to. When Phileas brought it up the other night, he made a good point. There will be those that think there's money to be had, and they'll come looking for it. If we're all working, they'll be less likely to think there is any."

"But there is," Wallis countered.

"Yes," Irving said. "But we don't know how much. For all we know, both Mother and Father will cut us off once they find out we've married Americans."

"I won't let that happen," Phileas announced.

His brothers gathered around him. "Jolly good of you," Conrad said. "But we don't know what Mother and Father will do."

Phileas' eyebrows shot to the ceiling. "Don't we?"

"Okay, Mother will do whatever it takes to make us miserable for a time, even if that means talking Father into disinheriting the lot of us."

Sterling raised a hand to silence them. "This is not the place to discuss our private matters." He stared at Oliver a moment. "You help Phileas. The rest of us are going to look at the future bakery. Phileas, make a list of what you need us to do here the rest of the week to help you." Without another word, they left Oliver and Phileas to their work.

"Well," Phileas said. "That was abrupt."

"He has a lot on his mind. They all do." Oliver picked up some discarded wallpaper and put it in a bucket. "I think Wallis would make an excellent teacher."

Phileas smiled. "So would you."

Oliver blushed. "Perhaps, but I still think one has to have some sort of paper that says you're qualified to teach."

"Perhaps." He studied him a moment. "Now that you're done with school, what will you do?"

"Whatever Father wishes, I suppose. He'll want me

to help him manage the estate. In short, I'll wind up as your secretary and accountant one day."

Phileas put an arm around him. "I can think of no one better. But if you want to do something else, then do it."

"But Father always talked about my managing..."

"I know he did," Phileas interrupted. "But I think that was Father's way to keep you around." He smiled warmly and got back to work. As the youngest, Oliver held a special place in their father's heart. All of them were aware of it, but no one minded. It was a common thing among families. Still, he wanted Oliver to do what appealed to him, not what pleased their father. Convincing Oliver of that, however, might take some doing.

Chapter Ten

Dora made chicken soup and biscuits for lunch. She wasn't sure what to do for dinner as her mind was full of thoughts of Phileas. If she didn't get him out of her head soon, she'd get nothing done.

She put a batch of cookies in the oven. If anything, Oliver would be happy and maybe distract her from his brother. The two were in the lobby, peeling off little scraps of wallpaper she and Phileas missed yesterday and preparing the room for the fresh paper. It was going to look wonderful, and she couldn't wait for it to be done. Phileas didn't mention a border, and she'd have to remember to ask him about one later.

If they could get the lobby papered in the next day or two, then she'd be happy. Then they'd tackle the dining room, and unless Phileas stayed on a while longer, she'd have to talk his brothers into helping her with the guest rooms.

She stirred her soup, took a taste, then added a little salt and pepper. The day was warm, but not too warm for soup. She loved making her mother's recipe and knew it was good. Besides, she hadn't made it for the Darlings and hoped they liked it. She already knew Mr. Hawthorne would. He liked anything she set in front of him.

Oliver slipped into the kitchen from the dining room and sniffed the air. "Ah, lovely. Cookies!"

She laughed. "Yes, sugar cookies to be exact. Now shoo." She made a show of waving him out of the kitchen.

"But are they done?"

"No, I barely put them in the oven. Off with you."

He groaned in protest and smiled.

"Stop playing around," she scolded.

He laughed and left. When she turned around, Phileas stood behind her. "Oh!"

Phileas smiled. "Sorry, I didn't mean to scare you."

Her hand to her chest, she took a few breaths. "Goodness gracious, but you did." She looked at the door to the hall. He must have slipped through it as she waved Oliver out the other. "Did you need something?"

"When is lunch?" He eyed the pot on the stove and made a beeline for it.

"Why?" she laughed. "Are you hungry?"

"Famished." He took off the lid and inhaled. "Mmm, smells good." He turned to her. "Chicken soup?"

"Yes. My mother's recipe."

He smiled and returned the lid. "We're ready to wallpaper."

She smiled and, for some reason, blushed. Maybe it was the 'we', but he meant Oliver, not her. "Good, I'm glad to hear it." She went to the stove and peeked in the oven, though there was no need to. She was trying to distract herself. Doggone, did he have to be so handsome?

"Well, I'd better get along so Oliver doesn't complain."

"That you're not doing your share of the work?" she teased.

"Something like that." He smiled again and left the kitchen.

The urge to follow him was overwhelming. But what good would it do? She'd be standing off to one side, twiddling her thumbs and watching them work. She didn't have time to help today – she had chores to catch up on from yesterday.

Dora left the kitchen to set the tables. She never knew who would be there for lunch but had a feeling everyone would show up today. As she worked, she thought of what her life was going to be like after Phileas and his brothers dispersed. Sterling would be at Letty's, Conrad at Cassie's and so on.

She sighed. Phileas and Oliver would have gone home

117

to England weeks beforehand. Would she ever see them again? They'd visit, wouldn't they? After all, wouldn't it be easier for them to come here than for say, Sterling and Letty and who knows how many children to travel to England? Could they even afford it? She didn't think so. She could only imagine how much money it cost the Darlings to travel here all the way from England, not to mention everything they were buying to fix up the town.

Done with the tables, she returned to the kitchen to put the soup in a tureen. The biscuits were in the warming oven, and she had just enough time to take care of another batch of cookies before everyone began filing in.

As soon as she put more cookies in the oven, Dora brought the soup to the table. "Lunch is ready," she called to the men.

Phileas put down the roll of wallpaper in his hand, then entered the dining room with a smile. "I can't wait."

Oliver followed. "Neither can I. Whatever is in that tureen smells good." Conrad sauntered into the dining room and joined them.

"I'll get the biscuits," she said and left for the kitchen. Would Letty or Cassie join them? What was she going to do when all this ended? Who was she going to share a meal with? Alma, Etta?

She brought the biscuits to the table and tried not to think about it. Every time she did, she got a hollow feeling in her gut. She didn't like it and knew it was only a matter of time before it made her curl up in a ball at night.

"Biscuits," Conrad exclaimed happily. "I do love biscuits with soup."

Cassie soon joined them, and Phileas said the blessing. She had no idea where Sterling, Wallis, or Irving were.

Mr. Hawthorne, on the other hand... "Sorry I'm late!" He hurried into the dining room and practically skidded to a stop. After taking a seat he smiled at everyone, then served himself. "I'm going to be ordering some things for my store soon. You gentleman wouldn't mind helping me set a few things up, would you? I can pay you." He took a spoonful of soup and rolled his eyes in pleasure. "Miss Jones, this is heavenly."

She blushed and nodded at the biscuits. "Help yourself to some of those. There're cookies for dessert."

"Splendid." He grabbed a biscuit. "Well gentlemen, what do you say?" He reached for the butter crock, his smile still in place.

"Of course, we'll help you," Conrad said. "But we need to help Dora first."

Mr. Hawthorne looked at her. "Oh, yes, the wallpapering."

"Among other things," Phileas said. "I'm afraid you'll have to discuss your business with Conrad and the rest of my brothers."

Mr. Hawthorne looked somber. "Are you looking

forward to returning to England?" He slathered his biscuit with butter then took a generous bite.

Phileas watched him a moment. "Yes, and no." He looked at her, and she sucked in a tiny breath as her heart leaped. She wasn't sure if he noticed or not as he got back to eating and said nothing more.

Dora ate in silence as Oliver spoke with Conrad about something. She ignored their conversation and tried not to look at Phileas every five seconds. At this rate, everyone would think she was sweet on him whether or not she was.

As soon as the meal was over (thank goodness!), she gathered the dishes and scurried into the kitchen. Trying not to be around Phileas or show interest in him was more taxing than she thought. Her heart was skipping, her belly fluttering, and she kept getting these funny little tingles up her spine.

Oliver snuck into the kitchen and went straight to the cookie jar. "I thought you came in here to get this. When you didn't come back, I decided to help you out." He gave her a boyish grin and she rolled her eyes.

"Go ahead, take what you want then put the jar on the table. If anyone wants some, they know where to find it."

"*I* know where to find it," he said. "The rest take some only because the jar got put in front of them." He waggled his eyebrows then left; the cookie jar tucked under one arm.

Dora smiled. It was a wonder he didn't follow her

into the kitchen when she excused herself to take out the second batch. She had enough dough to make a third, so she got to work.

As she spooned dough onto the cookie sheet, she thought of what her life was like before Phileas and his brothers came along. She and Pa had a simple life, as did most folks in Apple Blossom. They worked, ate, slept, then did it all over again, but the pace was leisurely and even though no one in town had a lot, that was okay. No one really cared other than Agnes. But as there were no other people in town with a lot of money, she had little to complain about.

Then the incident happened, and everything changed. Still, what would she be doing if the Darling brothers hadn't stumbled upon Apple Blossom one day?

Dora looked around the kitchen and sighed. "Starving, that's what." she sighed and continued to drop dough onto the sheet. It was a good thing she was set now for a time. Between their long stay and the small loan she got to work on the hotel when they arrived, she could breathe easy. Problem was, she'd be alone.

The next day Phileas went downstairs to the kitchen for a cup of coffee, said good morning to Dora, then slipped out the back door. He wanted to breathe the fresh morning air before the day really got started. He liked it here, and enjoyed the sweet smells of Apple Blossom, not to mention the sweet scent of a certain innkeeper. If he wasn't careful, he was going to have a hard time leaving.

A sound caught his ear, and he looked toward the captain's barn and the meadow beyond. Captain Stanley was hitching his horse to his wagon. "Now where could he be off to?" Curious, he strolled that way to find out. "Good morning," he called when he was close enough.

Captain Stanley scowled at first, then smiled. "Phileas, lad. What brings you here?"

He waved at McSweeny, the captain's horse. "I was just wondering where you were off to."

The captain gave him an exaggerated roll of his eyes. "Virginia City for a few supplies and some recreation." He chuckled then looked around. "I keep forgetting who my passenger is."

Phileas laughed then shook his head. "I'm not following you."

The captain cackled. "Well, the old windbag finally gave poor Francis permission to take a little trip with me to Virginia City. We're going fishing."

He smiled. "Well, now, that is news. I wonder what made her change her mind. I heard she was dead set against it."

The captain shrugged. "Well, maybe with Mr. Hawthorne here, he being an educated man, she feels culture has finally come to Apple Blossom."

His jaw went slack. "What? My brothers and I are from England."

"Yes, but you're leaving."

His eyebrows shot up. "Not all of us."

The captain smiled. "Glad to hear it. Agnes will bust a gut. She's under the impression you'll all go."

"Then won't she be surprised." Phileas shook his head in annoyance. "That woman."

"Sea hag."

Phileas smiled. "That too."

The captain finished what he was doing, then climbed onto the wagon seat. "Well, wish us luck. Poor Francis is afraid she'll say something at the last minute and he won't be able to go, but so far so good."

He smiled. "I wouldn't worry too much. Maybe Agnes is beginning to realize that having a few new folks in town will help it thrive."

"Let's hope." He gave the horse a slap of leather and the wagon lurched forward. Despite the early morning, a little cloud of dust rose behind the wheels and Phileas watched it dissipate into the air. Would it be a hot summer? He'd never thought to ask anyone about the summer weather. Probably because he knew he wouldn't be here.

With a sigh he returned to the hotel and breakfast. Once seated, the food on the table made his mouth water. Dora had made scrambled eggs, bacon, and fried potatoes. It was a far cry from toast and kippers, but he didn't care. He liked the American version of breakfast. Hearty.

As soon as he said a quick blessing, everyone began to eat. Phileas mused on who would say the blessings after he was gone but pushed the thought aside. He didn't want to think about anything having to do with his leaving. He had the hotel to worry about and that was enough.

Sterling looked at him a moment. "Where were you?"

"Yes," Irving said. "You came down late."

"On the contrary, I was out back speaking with the captain."

"And how is Captain Stanley this morning?" Dora asked.

He met her gaze and swallowed hard. "Off to fish with Mr. Featherstone."

Conrad dropped his fork. "What? I thought fishing with the captain was akin to a night of frolic in a brothel to Agnes."

"That's what she thinks the captain will do to her poor Francis," Sterling said.

"She relented?" Oliver said in shock. "What's the matter with her?"

Phileas shrugged. "Maybe she decided it was time she let the man have a day or two to himself. Perhaps he's been cranky lately."

"Could be," Dora said. "Poor Mr. Featherstone never gets to do anything by himself. Agnes is on him all day, all night."

Irving shuddered. "Horrible woman."

Sarah made a face. "I admit, she's not my favorite person in town."

Flint made a face to rival his mother's. "She's mean."

"That's enough about Agnes," Dora said. "We talk anymore about her, and we'll spoil our breakfast."

Lacey clutched her doll to her chest and looked around the table. "Why is Mrs. Featherstone so grumpy?"

Phileas smiled. "Some people, no matter how much they have, are never happy."

Lacey frowned. "But if you have everything you want, wouldn't that make you happy?"

He sat back in his chair and looked at his brothers. "Sometimes it's not about having everything you want as far as possessions, Lacey, but more about the people in your life. Take Mrs. Featherstone, for example. She has no children as far as I know." He glanced at Dora.

"She doesn't. But all her siblings do." Dora smiled at Lacey and Flint. "Agnes isn't lucky like your mother."

"How is Ma lucky?" Flint asked.

"She had you." Dora picked up her fork and got back to eating as Flint and Lacey smiled at their mother.

Phileas fought the urge to watch her eat. Did she want children? His eyes flicked to Hawthorne and back. Egad, would she have them with him?

When breakfast was finished, he helped Dora clear the table and take the dishes to the kitchen. He didn't say a word, but just wanted to be near her a few minutes longer before he and Oliver started the wallpapering. He wanted to get as much of the lobby done today as he could. If things stretched into tomorrow, so be it.

He set the dishes in the sink, then took the kettle

from the stove to fill it. Maybe he could talk to Dora while the water heated. That would give him a few more minutes...

Back inside, Dora stood in front of the sink, waiting. "You don't have to help me," she said. "I know you and Oliver have a lot of work to do."

He looked into her eyes. "Yes."

She swallowed hard. "You... should put the kettle on the stove."

He looked at it. He was still holding the kettle? Well, what do you know? He set it on the stove then looked at the door that led to the hall. "Well, I ought to go."

She nodded, her eyes roaming his face. "Yes, you should."

Phileas slowly stepped toward the door, got halfway there, then practically bolted through it. Once in the hall he took a deep breath. "Goodness."

"What?" Oliver asked. "Where's the water? Don't we need it to make the wheat paste to put the wallpaper up?"

"I'll fetch us some momentarily. Right now, I need to catch my breath."

"Why?"

He turned to the door. "Because I'm... oh, never mind." He went to the staircase and sat. "Ollie, you're supposed to be making sure I don't do anything stupid."

Oliver laughed. "You said make sure you don't fall in love."

"Precisely."

Oliver glanced down the hall. "What did you do?"

"Nothing, but... every time I'm around her of late my heart beats like a drum, I break out in a sweat, and I can't think straight."

Oliver gasped. "No."

"Yes! So will you kindly do your job?"

Oliver joined him on the stairs. "Tsk-tsk, brother. You're going to have to be more careful."

"And you're going to have to be more observant. I could have helped her clear the table then kissed her at the sink."

"You didn't, did you?" Oliver gasped. "Phileas!"

He pinched the bridge of his nose. "I did nothing of the kind. I was merely using that as an example."

Oliver fanned himself.

"Oh, stop," Phileas scolded. "I'm serious."

He left the stairs. "You aren't really falling in love, are you?" He paced back and forth a few times. "You can't, Phileas. You just can't."

He nodded sympathetically. "I know. Don't worry, I'll keep my heart in check. Just keep an eye out in case you see me doing something I ought not to be doing."

"Like what?"

He laughed half-heartedly. "Like be in the same room with Dora." He left the stairs and slapped Oliver on the back. "Let's get to work."

Oliver gaped at him. "How am I to do that?"

He sighed. "I don't know, but I hope you think of something."

Chapter Eleven

As soon as Dora finished with the dishes, she did a little mending, then scooted across the street to Alma's. She needed nothing other than some conversation. Or anything to distract her from Phileas.

She entered the building and found Alma staring at her wall of tools and nails and other hardware. "Morning, Alma."

She didn't turn around. "Uh-huh."

"What?"

"Yes, it is. I guess." Alma glanced her way. "It all depends on how you look at it." She crossed her arms and blew a wisp of red hair from her face. "Gone. This will soon be gone." She arched an eyebrow and faced Dora. "Or will it?" She spun on her heel and marched to her post behind the counter.

Dora stared after her. Alma would not be in the

mood for much conversation. She was obsessed with Mr. Hawthorne's hardware store. "Um, so, have you seen him the last couple of days?"

Alma grabbed her feather duster and began dusting the counter. "I have no idea who you're referring to."

Dora rolled her eyes. "Come now, you know perfectly well. Has Mr. Hawthorne been in here?"

She glanced at the ceiling. "Hmm, you tell me. Has he had any reason to leave the hotel? I don't think so." She got back to dusting, then paused. "Oh, unless it's going through with his ridiculous idea of setting up a hardware store down the street from me." She furiously worked her way across the counter. "Nope, haven't seen him."

Dora sighed and watched Alma go back and forth from one end of the counter to the other. Land sakes, was she going round the bend? "It's not that bad," she consoled. "Personally, I think you're looking at this all wrong. His store will only help yours."

Alma started dusting the shelves behind her. "It will? A good part of my business comes from hardware, and he'll take that from me."

Dora leaned against the counter and thought a moment. "Only because the Darlings have been giving it to you. If they hadn't come to town, how much business would you lose?"

She stopped dusting. "I...I'm not sure."

"See?" Dora went around the counter and took the duster from her. "You must remember, the only reason

you're making money is because of Phileas and his brothers. As soon as he's done with the hotel and leaves, then
it's only a matter of finishing up a few things. Then
everything will be back to normal. Remember what I
said?"

Alma's face screwed up in confusion. "I'm afraid
not."

"Who does most of the shopping in this town?"

Alma nodded sheepishly. "The women."

"And who would benefit most if you got rid of a lot
of your hardware and carried more things for the
women?"

Alma hung her head. "I would."

Before Dora could comment, the bell over the door
rang and in walked Mr. Hawthorne. Great. Could his
timing be any worse? With any luck, he wouldn't get
poor Alma riled up. Dora watched as he went straight to
the hardware section.

Alma squared her shoulders and cleared her throat.
"Can I help you?"

He glanced at her then fixed his eyes on the bins of
nails. "Not at the moment." He whipped a small pad and
pencil out of his jacket pocket and began jotting things
down.

Dora and Alma exchanged the same look of confusion. "What are you doing?" Alma asked.

"Research." He scribbled a few more things on the
pad then went to a wheelbarrow. "How much are you
charging for this?"

Alma's jaw dropped as her eyes widened. "Are you writing down my prices?"

He shrugged. "Something wrong with that?"

Dora pinched the bridge of her nose. "Oh, dear."

Alma wasn't so calm about it. "What? You're spying on me!"

"Not at all," he said. "I'm merely doing some research into the pricing strategies of hardware in a small community."

Alma's jaw dropped a second time. "Spying."

He smiled. "Research."

She strode up to him and Dora thought she might slap him. Instead, she got in his face. "*Spying.*"

He took a few steps back. "How often do you have to order nails?"

She narrowed her eyes and pointed at the door. "If you're not here to shop, then leave."

He glanced between the door and the nails. "Very well." He went to the bins and studied them. "I'll need three pounds of these, that wheelbarrow over there, three hammers... no, make that four. A saw, a ladder, and..." He tapped the pencil against his chin a few times. "... a shovel." He smiled. "That ought to do it."

Alma gaped at him. "You're actually buying things?"

"Of course. You're the only store in town." He went to the counter. "Do I need to write any of that down for you?"

Alma glanced at Dora. "What should I do?"

131

Dora bit her lip to keep from laughing. "See to his list."

Alma glared at Mr. Hawthorne, then got to work. It had to gall her to be gathering things he would use to build his hardware store... wait a minute.

Dora came alongside him. "What do you need all this for? Aren't you renting the building up the street?"

"Yes, but I need to build shelves. I'm off to the feed store next to purchase some lumber. Then I'll enlist the help of the Darlings. With that many men working, I'll have the place ready in no time."

She nodded then went to help Alma.

Alma brought a few sacks to the nail bins. "What sizes?"

He perused the selections. "One pound of large, one medium, and better give me a pound of the small."

She began scooping nails into a sack as Dora and Mr. Hawthorne watched.

"So," Dora began. "Are you planning on carrying more than what Alma offers here?"

"Of course. I'll have everything a person needs to build a house. Plus parts for farm equipment, harness and horse tack, and other items. Guns, for example."

Alma stopped, stared at him wide-eyed a moment, then got back to work.

Dora saw the mix of horror and anger in her eyes and had to think of what might put such a look on her face. She didn't even sell guns. Dora glanced around the store

132

and spied the catalogue sitting by the cash register. If Alma didn't carry it, she could order it. But if Mr. Hawthorne carried things like pistols and rifles in his store, then Alma would lose part of her catalogue business as well. She made little off it, but it was more business lost.

She looked at Alma, who was filling the last bag of nails. No wonder she felt threatened. "What else will you carry in your store?"

"Oh, let me see. Lanterns, kerosene, oil, a few household goods."

"Household goods!" Alma cried. She sucked in a breath then carried the bags of nails to the counter. Her jaw was tight, and Dora could see she was doing her best to control her temper.

"Did I say something wrong?" Mr. Hawthorne asked innocently.

"Well," Dora began, "you can carry what you want in your store, but wouldn't you have more room for tools if you didn't carry household items?"

He nodded. "I hadn't thought of that."

"And if you don't carry it, Alma will. You can send folks here."

He eyed Alma.

"And the same goes for the general store. What Alma doesn't carry; she can send the customer to you. If you work together, then you'll both have happy customers." Dora's eyes flicked between them.

"There's a lot of truth to what you say," Mr.

Hawthorne said. "What do you think, Miss Kirk? We work together to put the customer first?"

Something between a growl and a laugh escaped her. "I'll go fetch your ladder." She stomped to the back of the store.

Dora shrugged. "Well, it was worth a try."

Mr. Hawthorne stared at the door leading to the back of the building. "Indeed." His head tilted as his face softened. "Indeed, it was."

Phileas had one entire wall done and took a break. They'd worked non-stop for an hour, and he hadn't realized how sore he was from the last two days. No matter —at least he had Oliver to help him.

"It looks good," Ollie commented as they stepped back to admire their work. "Don't you think so?"

Phileas nodded. "Beautiful."

Dora stood just inside the dining room and stared at the wall with the lobby's front windows. "Oh, Phileas, you're right, the green is lovely."

He smiled at her, then nodded at the wall. "You'll need to pick out a border."

"I'm surprised you hadn't already." She crossed the lobby to where they stood and admired their work. "I can't wait to see the room when it's finished."

Oliver backed up and went down the hall toward the kitchen.

Phileas shook his head. "He's heading for the cookie jar."

"I know."

He smiled. "Our mother used to complain about the number of biscuits and sweets Ollie consumed. She probably hasn't known what to do with herself since we've been gone."

"Then she'll be happy when you return." She looked at him, sadness in her eyes.

His heart lurched at the sight, and he stepped back. "We'll start another wall in a moment. I thought it best we take a break."

She turned to face him. "Thank you," she said softly.

He nodded. "It's my pleasure. You know that."

Dora looked at the floor. "I do know. You love this." Her head came up. "Will you continue this kind of work when you get back to England?"

A half-hearted laugh escaped him. "If only I could. Unfortunately, our regular work will resume, and my life will be filled with any number of ledgers and roofs that need fixing, broken equipment, seeing to livestock and all sorts of other matters." He left off the part about caring for a large estate, never mind all the other obligations a viscount had. But it could be years before he had to take it on. Until then he'd assist his father in the day-to-day running of the estate to make sure he could handle things when the time came.

"I'll make some tea. Would you like a cup?" Dora headed down the hall.

He followed. "That sounds lovely. And if we're lucky, Oliver left us some cookies."

She smiled as they entered the kitchen to find Oliver at the worktable, a cookie in his hand. Phileas went to the cookie jar and took one. "Thank goodness, there's still a few left."

"How thoughtful," Dora tacked on. She took one for herself, then set about getting what she needed. Phileas had filled the kettle when she went to Alma's. It was always good to keep the kettle filled around here.

Soon they were seated around the kitchen table sipping tea and enjoying cookies. "Oliver, if you don't stop eating these," she said, "there won't be enough for dessert tonight."

He smiled between bites. "Then you'll have to make more."

She shook her head. "You need to learn to make them."

He grinned. "You'd teach me?"

"Why not?"

"Oh, no, don't," Phileas lamented. "He'll turn into a mad baker and be worthless to the rest of us."

"And I'd eat them all," Oliver laughed.

"That too." Phileas took the last cookie and shrugged. "I suppose it wouldn't hurt to learn." He took a bite, chewed and swallowed. "You've had to work extra hard to feed us, Dora. The least we can do is bake a few batches of cookies."

She giggled. "Yes, but you're the ones eating all of them."

"But at least you wouldn't have to do all the work," Oliver pointed out.

She sighed. "That's true."

Phileas smiled, put his hand on her arm and looked into her eyes. "I know we're paying customers here, but if you'd give us a few cooking lessons, we could make you dinner."

"We could?" Oliver said.

Phileas caught his shocked expression. "It will be good for us to learn a thing or two about cooking. You can surprise Mother with your culinary skills when we return." His eyes never left Dora's, and he noted the sadness in them when he mentioned returning. Did she not want them to leave? Or was it him alone?

"I'm not sure I want to subject my kitchen to that." She pulled her gaze from his and went to the stove. "Does anyone want more tea? I could make another pot."

Phileas sighed. He enjoyed watching her at the stove, be it cooking, baking, or just heating water. There was a hominess to the sight that warmed his heart and made him want to stay. But it wasn't meant to be. Instead, he'd have to suffer through all the women his mother was sure to parade in front of him the moment he got home.

"Anyone?" she prompted.

"I could do with another cup." Oliver eyed the cookie jar. "When did you want to give me a baking lesson?"

She turned to them with a smile. "How about when you finish the lobby?"

Oliver gave him a pleading look. "Phileas?"

He fought an eye roll. "Oh, please. You're not a child, Ollie."

Oliver grinned like a loon. "But it's cookies. Can you imagine the stir I'll cause at home if I take to baking?"

He cringed. He could imagine it all right. Their mother would have a conniption, not to mention their cook. "While you're here, you can bake all you want."

Oliver grinned in satisfaction. Humor was his way of dealing with an unpleasant situation and Phileas didn't wonder if he was having second thoughts about going home. In reality, Oliver could stay if he wanted and return later. Phileas was the one that had to go back, if only to explain what happened to the rest of his brothers. Still, it wouldn't be pleasant and would cause more than a "stir," as Ollie put it. It would be an outright scandal. He could imagine the rumors flying through the county now.

"If no one minds," Dora said. "I'm going to have another cup, then check on Alma."

Phileas blinked a few times. "What? Is something wrong?"

"Mr. Hawthorne came into the general store while I was there, and poor Alma was fit to be tied."

Phileas glanced at Oliver and back. "What did he do?"

She spooned tea into the pot. "He was looking to see

what she charged for different things, writing them down, then informing her of the goods he'd carry in his hardware store. Of course, part of it was my fault. I asked him questions about his store, and he answered. Much to Alma's dismay." She looked sheepish as she began pouring hot water from the kettle into the pot.

"Alma's still upset?" Oliver asked.

"Oh, yes." Dora returned the kettle to the stove. "She's convinced he's going to steal all her business, including orders from the catalogue."

"But she makes no money from that," Phileas pointed out. "I know because I ordered quite a bit. She takes a small percentage to cover her cost of storing the goods and the post."

"True, but when Mr. Hawthorne announced he'd carry items folks would usually order, she..." Dora sighed. "... didn't like it."

"Did she throw something at him?" Oliver asked. "Father told me that when women are really upset, they throw things."

Phileas shook his head. "Father tends to exaggerate."

"Not with this. He told me he had personal experience." Oliver's eyebrows shot up. "Oh, wait..."

"Yes," Phileas said. "I suggest *you* wait, and we'll have a conversation about *that* another time." He turned back to Dora. "I think Alma needs some reassurance that her store will be okay. After all, she'll carry a lot more items than he will."

"That's what I keep trying to tell her, but it doesn't sink in."

"Maybe we should shop more," Oliver suggested.

Phileas smiled. "Yes, and we'll start by shopping for some wallpaper border." He smiled at Dora. "Right?"

She smiled back. "Right."

Chapter Twelve

By the time Dora was done baking a couple batches of cookies, Phileas and Oliver had completed their wallpapering. They'd had a quick lunch earlier and discussed their plan of action. Thankfully, Mr. Hawthorne whipped in, grabbed some sandwiches, and hurried back to the building he was fixing up. He asked again about getting help from the other Darlings, and Phileas told him he should discuss things with Sterling at dinner.

Now the three were ready to venture across the street to Alma's. She and Phileas would pick out a border for the lobby while Oliver shopped for souvenirs to take back to England.

When they reached the general store, Alma was on the front boardwalk eyeing the buildings up the street. More specifically, Mr. Hawthorne's. "What are you doing?" Dora asked.

Alma spun to face them. "Nothing." She stood, her hands clasped behind her back, and twisted back and forth in an obvious attempt to look innocent.

"Really?" Dora replied. "Because I could have sworn you were watching Mr. Hawthorne helping Mr. Atkins unload a wagon of lumber."

Alma's eyebrows shot up. "Oh?" She turned around and looked in their direction. "Well, I'll be. Mr. Atkins *is* helping Mr. Hawthorne with some lumber." She turned around and smiled. "How very boring. Need something?" She headed for the door.

Dora shook her head in annoyance and followed her inside. "We're here to look at wallpaper borders."

Alma nodded at Phileas. "He ordered some." She bit her lower lip. "Was it okay to say that?"

Dora's face screwed up in confusion as she turned to Phileas. "You did? I thought I had to pick some out and if there wasn't a good match, order some."

He made a face, then smiled. "Well, I may have ordered a few rolls in hopes they'd match my earlier selections. But the choice is still yours."

Alma nodded and smiled. "He did. They're all lovely. Would you like to see them?"

Dora shook her head at Phileas but smiled. "I would." He'd thought of everything—and so early on too. She was grateful and wished he'd stay longer.

"I'll be right back." Alma went to the storeroom.

"What shall I do?" Oliver asked forlornly. "I haven't

any idea what to get Mother and Father, let alone the rest of the household."

"You know everyone well enough," Phileas pointed out. "Start shopping."

Oliver breathed a sigh and began to look around.

"You haven't been picking up souvenirs for your family during your trip?"

Phileas gave her a sheepish look. "In case you haven't noticed, we've been preoccupied. But better we get things here than in some fancy store in San Francisco."

Oliver brought a small bottle of perfume to them. "What about this?" He handed it to her. "You're a woman, what do you think?"

She pulled out the stopper and took a cautious sniff. "Not bad. Smells like lilacs."

Oliver took a long whiff, shut his eyes tight while making a face, and shoved the stopper inside. "Mother will love it."

Phileas laughed. "How do you know? You don't seem to."

Oliver waved his hand in front of his face to clear the air. "Because when I hate a perfume she wears, she always loves it."

Phileas laughed. "Just like Father. That is amusing."

"Not for your father," Dora said.

Alma returned with some rolls of border and set them on the counter. "What do you think of these?"

Dora moved to examine them. "Oh, Phileas, did you pick this out to go with the paper we put up?"

He smiled and took a roll from her. "I picked patterns I thought would match. There's more than one that will work." He handed it back to her.

Dora examined one with cabbage roses and would match the green diamond patterned wallpaper perfectly. "This will look lovely."

"I haven't seen the lobby yet," Alma said. "Is it done?"

"Almost," Phileas said. "We'll finish tomorrow and put up the border."

"Is there enough?" Dora asked.

"I measured the room," he said. "Trust me, there will be plenty."

She smiled. He really had thought ahead. "Then I like this one." She gave the rose border back to Alma.

She smiled, set it on the counter, then went to fetch the rest.

Oliver wandered to another part of the store, leaving Dora alone with Phileas. She gave him a sidelong glance, then fingered the roll. "You have excellent taste."

He sighed. "I know."

Dora laughed. "And you're so modest."

He sighed again. "I know that too."

She blushed and tried to look at anything but him. Alma's store had taken on a more feminine look since Mr. Kirk died. Slowly but surely, she was making it her own. Good. She needed to. If Mr. Hawthorne's place catered mostly to men, then why shouldn't Alma's cater to the women in town?

Alma returned with the rest of the rolls and set them down. "Will there be anything else?"

Dora looked for Oliver, who was trying on different hats. "Would your father like one of those?" she asked Phileas.

He smiled. "He would. Especially if it came from Oliver."

Dora watched him put on a brown derby, take it off, and put on something a cowboy would wear. "What sorts of hats do people wear in England?"

"Not the sort Oliver is wearing. You don't see them."

"That would be because there are no cowboys," Alma teased.

"Right you are." Phileas smiled and leaned against the counter. "Oliver should get our father one. I think it would delight him."

"Then I'll suggest which one to get." Alma headed that way, a smile on her face.

"She's in a better mood now," Dora observed.

"Yes, I just hope it lasts." Phileas gazed into her eyes. "You're a good friend, Dora."

She forced a smile. "I'm not close with Alma. Not like I am with Letty and Jean."

"Still, you came here earlier because you knew she was distraught. And here you are again, trying to better her mood. That's commendable."

She crossed her arms. She never knew what to do when folks gave her a compliment. When they did, it was usually about her cooking or something to do with the hotel. It was never about her character.

He leaned in her direction. "It's okay to take a few pleasant words about yourself."

She blushed. "Thank you. It's just that Alma has no good reason to fear Mr. Hawthorne. Still, she feels threatened and that concerns me."

"I understand, but you can't let it bother you. Alma is alone, trying to survive just like you are. What it comes down to is people. If you have enough residents in town to support the local businesses, then things work. But you've lost people, either to the incident or they moved away because of it."

She noted the concern on his face and her heart melted. "All true. That's why Mr. Hawthorne's arrival is a good thing. If more people come, that means more business for all of us."

"Exactly. Now all we have to do is convince Alma of that." He stepped away from the counter. "Tell me, do you ever have town meetings?"

"Not since the incident. Why?"

"Perhaps you should. I know Irving has mentioned a few things the town could do to bring people here. Perhaps it's time to have a meeting and discuss them."

She nodded. He had a point. She could always do with more business. She would be fine for a while with the Darlings' extended stay, but soon they'd no longer be at the hotel, and then what? No guests, no money – it was as simple as that. "I'll speak to Mr. Featherstone when he gets back from his fishing trip with the captain."

He smiled. "Ah, yes. I wonder how he and the captain are faring."

Dora nodded. "I'm wondering how Agnes is doing while they're away."

"They'll be back this evening. You have between now and then to find out."

Dora nodded and realized she hadn't seen hide nor hair of Agnes for the last couple of days. What could she have been doing all this time?

Dinner was another quiet affair, Phileas noted. Probably because Hawthorne hadn't shown up yet—when he did, there would no doubt be some conversation. By this time everyone knew he wanted to speak to Sterling and the others about locking in some help with his hardware store. Everyone also knew that Alma wasn't happy about any of it, and no one knew what to do about that. She should be happy there was a new store in town, but she was getting more agitated by the day. What would she be like by the time he opened?

When Hawthorne did show up, he wore a happy face and sat at his usual spot. "Good evening, everyone." He perused the platters of food and licked his lips. "Miss Jones, this looks wonderful."

"Thank you." Dora took another bite of her chicken and dumplings.

Phileas watched her a moment then got back to eating. It was delicious. Everything she made was good and part of him was jealous that his brothers would continue to enjoy her cooking while he and Oliver went back to their normal fare.

He studied the food on the table. Chicken and dumplings, dinner rolls, salad, carrots. Yes, he was going to miss this. Miss the company too. He took another bite of the succulent chicken, savoring its taste as he glanced at Dora who sat across the table from him. He was going to miss *her*.

Hawthorne cleared his throat. "So I was wondering if I could talk to you all about the store." He hesitated and Phileas could feel the tension filling the room.

Sterling eyed him over his food. "Yes, we know, Mr. Hawthorne. Phileas mentioned you still wanted help and Conrad told me you'd like as many hands as you could get. Though I don't know why you'd need all of us to help."

"All of us?" Oliver said in surprise. "I thought he might need a few, but not all."

"It's an extensive project." Hawthorne said. "I have a lot of ideas, but none of them will work or become successful if the store isn't set up right. I need the help of everyone here to make sure things go smoothly."

There was a silence before Oliver spoke up again. "What kind of help do you need, Mr. Hawthorne?"

"Some advertising, for starters. Word about the hardware store needs to get out so people will start getting excited about it."

Irving laughed. "This is Apple Blossom. I assure you, the word is already out."

The rest of them chuckled but Hawthorne ignored them and continued to make his case. "I also need help with the books. I'll need to track my finances, so I can make sure I'm not overspending. I'm sure I can set up my own system, but one of you might see something I've overlooked. I also need help with the stocking and ordering of inventory. These are tasks that take time and manpower, so I'm hoping you all can help."

There was a long pause before Sterling finally spoke. "We all want to see your store succeed, but we've also promised to help finish the hotel, and it has to come first." He looked him over. "Just how big of a store are you planning to have? The books can't be that hard to do."

Hawthorne dragged them into a discussion on economics.

Phileas caught Dora's sigh of relief. He was glad his brother was willing to help. Now they just had to prove to Hawthorne that they could do it with half the manpower he wanted. When they were done with the hotel, they had Irving's building to tackle. His brother wanted to get the first floor ready so it could be up and running for Sarah's new business. He wished he could be here to see it, but knew he'd be gone by then.

Phileas pushed the thought of leaving out of his mind and continued eating. After a moment or two, he noticed the room grew quiet and glanced up to see Hawthorne smiling at him. "Did you need something?"

His smile grew. "You're a lucky man, having stayed in this cozy little town. I'll send you something from my new store once it's up and running."

Irving glanced around the table. "You want to send Phileas and Oliver something?"

Hawthorne nodded. "Why not?"

"To *England*?" Sterling said.

"Sure." Hawthorne began eating as the brothers exchanged quizzical looks.

Phileas couldn't help the pang of guilt that stirred in his stomach. But it had nothing to do with Hawthorne's strange offer. The idea of leaving his family and this town behind made him feel sick, but he knew it was something he had to do. Taking a deep breath, he excused himself from the table and went outside for some air.

As he stepped out, he heard a rustle behind him. Dora came through the hotel doors and joined him on the boardwalk. "Are you okay?" she asked, her eyes filled with concern. "Is there something you need?"

A shiver of fear and excitement ran up his spine. There was something about Dora's intensity that drew him to her, even though he knew he should stay away. "I have a lot on my mind and a lot to do." He shrugged. "I guess you could say I'm feeling overwhelmed."

"You don't have to help him, you know. You have too

much to do as it is." She took a step closer, and he gasped. "Are you sure you're all right?"

He held his breath and nodded. "Fine," he whispered.

Dora didn't look convinced. "You could stay."

He swallowed hard and looked into her eyes. She had no idea what she was doing to him. Good grief, neither did he! What *was* happening? His chest was warm, and he was getting all gooey inside. No, that wasn't right. Softer? Maybe. As if peace were seeping into his bones.

She leaned closer and smiled, her blue eyes sparkling with magic and mystery. Her lips looked so soft, he wanted to touch them with his own. He gulped just thinking about it.

Oh bother! Dora was beautiful like an angel, her skin pale and creamy, her hair dark and soft. Light from the lamp in the hotel window illuminated her face, bathing her in its glow. Her lips were full, soft, and inviting. And if he didn't high-tail it back inside pronto, he'd be in big trouble! "Er, our food is getting cold."

"But Phileas, are you going to be okay?"

Sure, nothing a jump in an ice-cold creek can't cure. "Of course." He started for the door. Oliver was shirking his duty! If he were out here instead of Dora, all would be well. But no! He was inside devouring chicken and dumplings, leaving him to the gaping jaws of love. Phileas had a strong feeling he'd get chewed up if he wasn't careful.

She brushed by him toward the hotel doors. She

smelled of roses and lavender, the scents of a summer meadow. Her perfume was delicate, sweet, and just enough to take his breath away. *Oliver! Help!*

Dora stopped at the doors and turned to face him. She said something, but he didn't hear what. He was too busy looking at her full, rosy lips and wanting to taste them. Was her kiss as sweet as her scent? He bit the inside of his cheek. "What was that?" He swallowed, his mouth suddenly dry. If they didn't go inside now, he was a dead man.

"I could give you a cooking lesson tomorrow if you like." She smiled and opened one door.

He openly gawked at her. It was as if he was seeing her for the first time. Her voice sounded like a low, melodic hum. It wasn't an annoying buzz and harbored no hint it could turn into a shrill scream like Agnes. That woman would make any man run for the hills. No, Dora's voice held a soothing tone that he wanted to hear again.

"Phileas?"

He jumped. That didn't come from Dora.

Sterling stood in the doorway, puzzlement on his face. "What is wrong with you?" He took Phileas by the shoulders and pulled him inside. "Do we need to talk?"

Phileas glanced at Dora. "Yes. Now, please." He grabbed Sterling's arm and ushered him toward the stairs. He couldn't risk another moment like this. If he did, his whole family might suffer.

Chapter Thirteen

Dora watched Phileas drag Sterling upstairs. What was going on? She left the lobby, went into the kitchen, and contemplated starting the dishes. Should she wait for him? It was the one time during the day she had Phileas to herself. She enjoyed their simple conversations about England, his brothers, the hotel, food, and anything that came to mind. She'd never spoken to a man like that before and found she liked it.

She returned to the dining room and began to clear the table. What she wouldn't give for some advice about now. Maybe she should speak to Captain Stanley when he returned from his fishing excursion. Hmm, could he be back already? Sometimes the captain took an extra day to return to town. And what about Agnes? She still hadn't seen her since the captain and Mr. Featherstone left.

She brought the dishes to the kitchen and got things ready, moving slowly hoping Phileas would come down and help her. But he didn't, and she wondered what he and Sterling could be talking about.

Dora started the dishes with a sigh. Time with Phileas was growing short. Should she spend as much time with him as possible, or try to stay away? She saw something tonight in the way he looked at her... she shook her head as she dried another dish. He had no interest in her and she saw not a hint of attraction in his eyes. How could there be? There hadn't been in all the time they'd spent together.

She was halfway through the dishes when Phileas entered. "You started without me?"

Was that disappointment in his voice? "Well, I wasn't sure how long you'd be. I couldn't wait too long."

He looked at the pile of plates she'd already done. "I'll put these away." He took the stack and headed for the hutch.

She watched him, her heart in her throat. Land sakes, she wasn't having feelings for him, was she? She swallowed hard. Okay, she was, but that didn't mean she was in love with him. In fact, she had plenty of time to make sure she didn't fall in love. Though she might need a little help.

She finished the dishes without incident, then tidied up the kitchen. Phileas watched her from the kitchen table and munched a cookie. She could feel his eyes on her and delighted in the little tingles going up her spine. But she had to remember that he was still leaving.

Done with the kitchen, she smiled. "Well, I guess I'll say goodnight." Good grief, was she blushing? She put a hand to her cheek to check, then quickly lowered it.

Phileas watched her, a slow smile forming on his face. "You look a little flushed. Is everything okay?"

She pressed her lips together. "Mm-hmm."

His smile grew. "Dora?"

She caught the sparkle in his eyes and smiled back. "It's nothing. I'm tired, that's all."

He stepped toward her. "So when you're tired, you make funny faces, is that it?"

"Mm-hmm."

Phileas laughed. "You're adorable when you're this way. Though I'm concerned that you're tired. You've worked hard the last few days. You should try to take it easy."

Now she laughed. "Hard to do when one runs a hotel."

He took another step. "I know. There's a lot of work to be done."

She crossed her arms. "You have no idea."

He closed the distance between them. "Dora, get some rest."

Her eyes closed. His voice was gentle, and more than a tingle went up her spine this time.

When she opened her eyes, he was standing before her. "Phileas," she whispered, "you should go."

He nodded, swallowed, then headed for the kitchen door leading to the dining room. *Was* he attracted to her? Dora wasn't sure, but it was clear she was becoming attracted to him. This was not good.

She hurried through the other kitchen door, down the hall and into her living quarters. Once her door was closed, she breathed a sigh of relief. This was going to be harder than she thought. In fact, she needed some help.

Dora put on her nightclothes, crawled into bed, then decided that first thing in the morning, she'd speak to her friends and ask for that help. She had no idea what to tell them, but she'd think of something. Heaven forbid she told them she was in love. That was the last thing she wanted to do. But she'd have to come up with something, and fast.

❧

The next morning Dora's plan had some substance. She'd speak to Letty, Cassie and Alma. Sarah was often busy with the children, so she didn't wish to involve her just yet. With any luck, she wouldn't need a fourth person.

She sat at her usual place at breakfast and, as soon as Phileas said the blessing, eyed Sterling across the table. "Is Letty coming to town today, or are you working at her place?"

"She's coming. She told me yesterday she had a few things to take care of."

"Would that involve a trip to the general store?" She

poked at her eggs, waiting for his answer. So far she'd avoided making too much eye contact with Phileas, but that couldn't last forever.

"It would, I helped her make a list last night."

"Good. I wanted to speak to Alma today and wouldn't mind some reinforcements."

Phileas cleared his throat. Had he noticed she wasn't looking his way? But the only reason he would was if he cared, which he didn't. She was trying to avoid losing her heart to him, so ignoring him shouldn't be a problem. For him.

"Someone should speak with her," Irving said. "She's blowing this Hawthorne business out of proportion."

Sarah looked around the table. "What do you mean?"

"She's overreacting," Sterling said. "She thinks..." He glanced at Mr. Hawthorne's empty chair. He'd taken a few muffins and hurried out the door earlier, determined to get as much work done on his place as he could before Sterling and some of the other Darlings helped him. "Well, she feels threatened by Hawthorne's store."

"Oh, dear," Sarah said. "That'll cause problems on both sides if she's not careful." She looked at Dora. "I'll help anyway I can."

Dora smiled back. "Thank you. I'll let you know if I need you."

Sarah smiled and got back to eating. As did everyone else. Dora took a bite of bacon and chewed slowly. She didn't want to upset Alma and thought that if she asked for her help, it would help take her mind off Mr. Hawthorne. She'd find out soon enough.

The meal over, everyone dispersed to take on their day. Including Phileas and Oliver, who headed straight for the lobby to finish it.

Dora cleared and washed the breakfast dishes, then headed for Alma's. Sarah and the children disappeared with Irving, and she guessed they were working on their new home today. Everyone was trying to wrap things up to take on the next project. Mr. Hawthorne was under the impression that was him. But his hardware store would have to wait.

She entered the store and went to the counter. "Alma?" There was no sign of her anywhere. She heard a loud thunk from overhead and looked up. Alma was in her living quarters.

Dora headed for the door leading to the back of the building. "Alma?" she called. "I'm coming up." She went up a set of stairs to a landing and knocked on the door. "Alma?"

The door opened. Alma brushed some of her red hair from her eyes and smiled. "Hello, did you need me to fill a list?"

"No, I came to ask a favor. But...I thought to wait until Letty came by."

"Oh?" She motioned her inside.

Dora stared at the furniture now sitting in the middle of the room." What are you doing?"

Alma stood next to her, hands on hips. "With all the wallpapering you're doing, I thought I'd change mine."

She looked around. She hadn't spent much time in the Kirks' living quarters and forgot what it was like. Alma had room, that's for sure. It was a quaint space and bright to boot. "What are you thinking?" She looked at the blue wallpaper covered with flowers. "Are you going lighter?"

"Yes, I'd like something in yellow. Wouldn't that look pretty?"

She smiled. "Indeed, it would. Need any help?"

Alma grinned sheepishly. "I was hoping you'd ask. Yes. I can use all the help I can get. The only time I have to work on my place is in the evenings after I close."

Dora nodded. "Has it been hard since your father died? Before there were the two of you to cover the store. Now there's only you."

Alma took one look at her, eyes misting, then broke into tears. Oh, dear. Her own problem would have to wait.

Phileas and Oliver stepped back to admire their handiwork. "There," Phileas said. "That doesn't look too bad."

"It's magnificent," Oliver commented. "You've outdone yourself."

"You helped."

"To put it up. But putting this together in your head. I couldn't do it." Oliver sighed. "I'm afraid I've not an artistic bone in my body. Such is life."

"No, but you're smart, Ollie. You have plenty to be proud of." Phileas put his arm around his brother. "Now I need to decide what to do next. But first, let's get the furniture back where it needs to be."

They got to work and soon had everything in its proper place. "What about the curtains?" Oliver asked.

"Yes, I have some all picked out. Alma has been holding them for me."

Oliver whistled. "I say, but how much did you spend on this place?"

"More than I care to share."

"It was all your traveling money, wasn't it?"

Phileas nodded. "Let us hope nothing happens on our return trip that requires a lot of funds. How are you set?"

"I still have money. We could get more, couldn't we?"

"Yes, but not without raising suspicions with Father, or Apple Blossom for that matter."

"You're right."

"Don't worry," Phileas assured him. "We'll be fine."

Oliver walked a large circle and studied the room. "Dora is going to love it."

Phileas smiled. "She already does." He sighed. "Speaking of love…"

Oliver cringed. "I know, I wasn't there for you last night. I'm sorry."

"How did you...?"

"I overheard you speaking with Sterling."

"Oh, I see." Phileas went to the nearest wall and knocked on it. "Thin, I guess."

"No, Sterling always keeps his door cracked open until right before he goes to bed."

Phileas laughed. "I'd forgotten about that. It's a good thing Dora didn't wander down the hall and overhear us." He stared at the floor. Maybe it would've been better if she had. With any luck, she'd avoid him the rest of his stay.

Once again, he resorted to the logic that if she was sweet on him, he'd know. But she'd shown no romantic interest in him or any of his brothers since they'd been in town. And of all the people they saw each day, they spent the most time with her: mealtimes, bumping into each other while going about their daily business, doing dishes...

"You look sad," Oliver said, breaking into his thoughts.

Phileas rubbed his face. "Do I? Frustrated is a better word. We're running out of time."

"Have you thought of sending a telegraph message to Mother and Father?"

Phileas went to the sofa and sat. "I have." He crossed his legs and rubbed his chin. "Often."

"Then what's wrong with doing so? It won't matter if we return a couple of weeks behind schedule. I think Father half expects us to."

"Perhaps you're right." Phileas got to his feet. "I'll speak to Sterling again. If we stay, we'll need more money. And that means sending a telegraph, anyway."

"Father will have no problem sending some, you know that."

"Yes, but when he does, then we return without the others, he will be upset."

Oliver had a knowing look. "But nothing like Mother."

Phileas shuddered. "No, I should say not."

They straightened up a few more things then went upstairs to wash up before going to Alma's. When Phileas came down, he noticed there was no sign of Dora. Was she still at the general store? Maybe Letty came to town, and the two were speaking to Alma. If that was the case, should he wait until this afternoon to get the curtains?

Oliver came downstairs. "What's the matter?"

Phileas held up a finger. "Wait here." He went to the kitchen to confirm Dora wasn't in the hotel. Sure enough, it was empty. "What are you and Alma doing?" She'd been gone over an hour. He returned to the lobby. "Let's fetch my curtains and put them up."

"Sure," Oliver said. "I just hope there's not a fight going on over there."

"Why do you say that?" Phileas headed for the hotel doors.

"Because I just saw Hawthorne go into Alma's store a few minutes ago."

Phileas froze a moment. "I say, that might not go well."

Oliver shrugged. "There's only one way to find out."

Phileas took a deep breath. "Let's go." He headed for the doors, opened them, then heard a woman scream. "Alma!" He hurried across the street.

Mr. Hawthorne came running out the store's front doors. He jumped off the boardwalk and into the street just as a vase came flying out after him, missing by inches. "What are you doing?" he yelled back. "Have you gone mad?"

Alma came out and wagged a finger at him. "You're not allowed in my store ever again!"

Phileas and Oliver exchanged a quick look. Oliver shook his head. "Father was right. They do throw things when they're angry."

Phileas rolled his eyes and headed for the store. "What's going on?" He looked at the shattered vase. "Alma, what are you doing?"

Her hands went to her hips. "That's none of your concern." She glared at Hawthorne. "And you! Stop coming in here and copying down my prices!"

"But it's only research," Hawthorne whined.

Phileas had no idea what was going on. The only person who could explain things to him at this point was Dora, and she was nowhere in sight.

Chapter Fourteen

Dora stood just inside the doors of the general store. Alma was on the boardwalk, yelling a warning at Mr. Hawthorne. They had been having a pleasant conversation when Alma heard the bell over the door downstairs. When she went down, the man was jotting things down in his pad again, which sent poor Alma round the bend.

She'd spoken about her feelings, and Dora tried her best to make sense of them. To her, there was no reason for Alma to feel so threatened by a hardware store. Though Mr. Hawthorne's odd behavior might be something else. He saw no problem in coming and writing down what Alma was charging for hardware items. But was he doing it to compete with her, or to keep the prices consistent for the townspeople? She hoped it was the latter.

Dora came outside, saw Phileas and Oliver in the

street with Mr. Hawthorne, and her heart leaped. But it wasn't because the two men looked like they were trying to shield him from another flying vase—it was because she was falling for him. She never got the chance to speak to Alma about her little problem and hoped she got one later. For now, she should think about making lunch. That is, if Mr. Hawthorne was safe now. "Alma, let's go inside."

Alma glanced over her shoulder. "Fine, but he's not allowed."

"But Miss Kirk," Mr. Hawthorne said, "I need supplies."

Alma narrowed her eyes again. "Too bad." She turned on her heel and stomped into the store.

Dora stood helplessly and shrugged at Phileas and Oliver. Mr. Hawthorne mumbled something about unreasonable women, then trudged up the street to his building. She followed Alma, not bothering to look and see where Phileas and Oliver were going. As soon as she was inside, she took Alma by the arm. "What do you think you're doing? You can't bar him from the store."

"Why not? I serve whom I want. And I don't want *him*."

Dora sighed. "Alma, be reasonable."

Her face fell. "That's just it. I can't. I don't know what comes over me. But every time that man comes in here, I just get so...so angry!"

Dora put her arm around her. "I'm sorry, I don't

understand what's happening. All I can do is try to help you through this."

Phileas and Oliver entered. "What happened?"

"Isn't it obvious?" Oliver quipped. "She doesn't want him in here."

"Yes, but why?"

Alma crossed her arms and stared at the floor. They weren't going to get anything out of her.

Dora steered her to the stool behind the counter. "Sit." She turned to the men. "Mr. Hawthorne keeps writing down the prices of Alma's hardware."

Phileas and Oliver exchanged a quick look. "What's wrong with that?"

"What's wrong with it?!" Alma jumped off the stool. "He's... he's spying!"

Phileas sighed then smiled at her. "Alma, if the man is going to open a store here, then he's going to want to keep his customers happy. He's probably making sure he doesn't overcharge them, while also making sure he doesn't, as they say, undercut you. Mr. Hawthorne won't wish to take business from you. He's merely giving people another opportunity to find what they want."

She stared at him open-mouthed. "Oh." She returned to the stool and hopped on it. "I see." She turned to the counter, rested her arms on it, then let her head fall onto them. "But I still think he's spying."

Dora tossed her hand in the air. "For the last time, he is *not* spying."

"Easy for you to say—this isn't your store. What if he

was opening a hotel?" Alma straightened and looked at her. "How would you like it if he came into your place and wrote down what you charged for your rooms?"

Dora glanced at Phileas. "It's not the same thing."

"It is. He'd be opening a business similar to yours."

Dora bit her lip. Okay, so Alma had a point. The town didn't need another hotel, and if by some miracle the hotel was nicer than hers, she'd be in trouble. "Everyone needs goods, Alma," she finally said. "Food, clothing, tools, not to mention games, books, fripperies."

"She's right," Phileas said. "These are everyday things. One doesn't need to stay in a hotel every day."

Alma slid off the stool. "Fine, I see your point." She pulled at her hair. "But that doesn't mean I have to like it!" She ran through the door to the back of the building and up the stairs to her living quarters.

Oliver looked at Phileas. "Does this mean we're not getting your curtains?"

Phileas pinched the bridge of his nose, then shook his head. "Oh, dear me." He smiled at Dora, making her heart leap in her chest. "I do have curtains."

She smiled. "They can wait. I think she might want to be alone." She motioned them to the door and stepped outside. Once the doors to the store were closed, she spoke. "I'm not sure what's going through her head, but this goes beyond competition. Not even Alma can explain it."

Oliver stepped off the boardwalk and looked at the

second-story windows. "Can she hear a customer if they come in?"

"She'll have her door opened a crack so she can hear the bell." Dora headed across the street. "Has anyone seen Letty?"

"No," Phileas said. "I don't think she's come to town yet."

"Probably because Sterling is there," Oliver said. "She'll probably come into town with him at lunchtime."

"Fine." She went into the hotel and stopped up short. "Oh, Phileas!" She smiled and turned a full circle. "This is lovely." Indeed, it was. The green wallpaper reminded her of an emerald. "I can't wait to have new guests."

"What about me?" Oliver said.

She smiled at him, gave him a hug, then stepped back. "Thank you so much." She turned to Phileas, who was blushing. "And you. I couldn't have done any of this without you." She hugged him too and, without thinking, gave him a kiss on the cheek.

His blush deepened. "You're welcome, m'lady." He bowed and straightened with a smile.

Now she was the one blushing. "Thank you." She didn't know why she thanked him again, other than to keep herself from throwing herself into his arms. He was tall, warm, and that simple hug was unraveling her resolve to keep her distance. Letty couldn't get here quick enough. She smiled. "Well, I'd better see to lunch. I

168

haven't the faintest idea what to prepare." She hurried for the kitchen.

"Dora, wait." Phileas caught up to her and followed her to the stove. "Dining room?"

She blinked in confusion. "What?"

"Shall we do the dining room next?" He closed the distance between them. "I think it best."

She stilled and didn't dare look at him. If she did, it might be her undoing. "Why, of course. Whatever you think."

They were so close they were almost touching. "I do," he said huskily, then cleared his throat. "I'd better see to those curtains." He went to the door, took one last look at her, then left.

Dora let go the breath she was holding. "Goodness." She went to the table and sat, her heart pounding and her knees wobbly. She sensed he'd wanted to put an arm around her, but why would he? She, on the other hand, might faint if he stood so close again. Land sakes, what was going to happen the next time they did the dishes?

Dora buried her face in her hands and tried not to think about it.

❧

Phileas entered the store slowly. He didn't expect Alma to throw a vase at him, but one never knew. If she thought he was Hawthorne, she might. "Hello?" He looked around. She must still be upstairs. He sighed and walked to the hardware section of the store. One wall had bins of nails and smaller tools. There was a wheelbarrow, a few shovels, a couple of picks and axes, and a handsaw. As he recalled, there was more last week. Hawthorne must have purchased things to help get his place set up.

He hoped the man didn't purchase tools thinking Sterling and the rest of his brothers would use everything. There was no guarantee the lot of them would lend a hand all at the same time. His priority was the hotel and would remain so whether or not Hawthorne needed help.

He went to the counter and ran a finger over the surface. There were a few small pockmarks and scratches, but the wood was still polished to a sheen. He looked at the half-open door that led to the back. Should he fetch his curtains without disturbing Alma? He'd already paid for everything and could leave her a note.

He was about to go into the back when Alma came through the door. She looked like she'd been crying. "Oh, Phileas. Hello." She went behind the counter and grabbed her trusty feather duster from a low shelf. "What can I do for you?" She began dusting the counter.

He tried to look sympathetic. "I came for my curtains."

"Oh, yes." She set the duster down, squared her shoulders and disappeared into the back.

He waited a few moments and looked around the store, trying to picture things in different places, where to add a splash of color.

When she returned, she held two large, wrapped packages. "I didn't think you'd want them getting dusty taking them across the street, so I wrapped them again. The paper they arrived in was torn, but the curtains are all right." She handed him the packages then went behind the counter and picked up the duster.

He watched her a moment, his heart going out to her. "Thank you." He wasn't sure what to say. Maybe he should let Dora know Alma had been crying and let her handle it. He was never worth much around a crying woman. What man was? "Well, I must be going. Thank you for re-wrapping the curtains. That was very thoughtful of you."

She smiled but said no more.

He went to the door, took a last look around the store, then left. When he got back to the hotel, he set the packages on the counter, then headed for the kitchen. Dora was at the stove, staring at it. "Trying to decide what to make?"

She turned to face him. "I don't know what to do to help her." She shook her head a few times. "I'm at a loss, Phileas. How can I help her?"

Against his better judgment, he closed the distance between them. "Dora, you've done what you can. Alma will have to figure it out on her own. I know she's upset, but like you, I'm not sure how to help her."

She nodded, looking sad.

Oh dear, she wasn't going to cry, was she? He hoped not. It was hard enough to see Alma looking teary-eyed, but Dora? He didn't think he could take it. "Sandwiches?"

She gave him a blank look. "What?"

"I'll help you make sandwiches." He went to the icebox. "What do we need?"

"Um..." She tapped her finger against her forehead. "Bread. I could use the chicken from last night, cut it up..."

His heart may have gone out to Alma, but it was running headlong at Dora. It was all he could do to stand there. He didn't dare get any closer lest he pull her into his arms. "Dora," he whispered. Great Scott, is that all he could manage? He sounded like he was about to pass out. Was he?

She went to the icebox and began taking things out. "Slice the bread."

"Right." Phileas went to the bread box, pulled out a loaf and got to work. If he stayed busy enough, maybe he wouldn't pull Dora into his arms and kiss her senseless. Maybe that would take the sadness from her eyes. He didn't think he could stand to see her this way again.

She brought what she needed to the worktable and set it down. "I have to run to Alma's. I need some mustard." She headed for the door leading to the dining room.

Phileas stopped her. "I can get it." He looked into her eyes and almost choked. She looked about to cry again. "Dora... are you okay?"

She swallowed hard. "Yes, I'm fine." She looked at the door. "Go."

He gave her a quick nod and left the kitchen. When he re-entered the store, he stopped to catch his breath. It was bad enough having to deal with Alma earlier, but he could hardly stand doing this with Dora. How was he going to get through the day?

"Alma, where's the mustard?" Phileas looked around the storefront. Once again, there was no sign of her. With a sigh, he began his search, found a jar, then went to the counter. "Alma?"

Silence.

"Oh, bother." He went through the door to the back and up the stairs to her living quarters. "Alma?" Phileas knocked on the door. There was no answer. "Where could she have gone?" He left, went back downstairs, and left some money on the counter. She might be down the street badgering Hawthorne. He hoped that wasn't the case. With any luck, she was apologizing instead.

Back at the hotel, he hurried into the kitchen with the mustard and set it on the worktable. "There." He tried to catch his breath. "I'm afraid Alma wasn't at the store."

"She might have gone for a walk. People know she takes her lunch about now." Dora finished slicing the bread and opened the jar of mustard.

Phileas noticed she'd already sliced up the leftover chicken and had it heating in a pan on the stove. "Ah, I was wondering how you were going to do this. I never would have thought to use leftover chicken and dumplings for sandwiches the next day."

"I've done it before, just not for you. It's quite good, but you must have mustard." She got back to work.

He sighed in relief. She seemed better now. "What else can I do?"

"Set the table, if you please." She smiled weakly and continued working.

"Right, the table." He smiled back and went to the hutch. Once he had a stack of plates, he took them to the dining room and got to work. There was no sign of Oliver and he wondered where he'd gotten to. No matter. He needed to concentrate on Dora. What was he going to do now? Every protective instinct he had was on high alert, and all she did was look like she was about to cry. Good grief, what would happen if she were in real danger? But she wasn't in danger now, he was. His heart was pounding and there was nothing he could do about it.

Finished with the plates, he returned to the kitchen to fetch some silverware. Dora didn't so much as blink in his direction. A good thing—he didn't think he could stand to see that sad look again.

Back in the dining room, he put the silverware on the table, then faced the kitchen door. What to do? If he stayed any longer than planned, he could wind up in some real trouble. His heart was about to commit mutiny, and he was inclined to let it.

He took a few deep breaths and let them out slowly.

He had to calm down if he could, then return to the kitchen and finish helping Dora. But the urge to hold her was winning out, and he didn't know what to do.

He looked at the ceiling. "Where are you, Oliver?" Fine, he'd go fetch him. He had to be upstairs. He crossed the lobby and took the stairs two at a time. "Some help you are, right when I need you most, you're not here." He reached Oliver's room and knocked. "Ollie?"

There was no answer. He rolled his eyes and opened the door. "Ollie, what are you...?"

Oliver wasn't in his room.

Phileas sighed. "Great, just great. I'm about to fall in love and there's no one here to stop me."

Chapter Fifteen

"...**A**nd then he has the audacity to come into my store and write what I'm charging for things." Alma took a bite of cookie and kept talking. "Who does he think he is?" She took the time to chew, thank goodness. Oliver was afraid she might choke.

Billy cast his line and took a bite of sandwich. No sooner had Phileas gone to the kitchen to see about lunch, Billy had walked into the hotel and wanted Oliver to go fishing with him. Who was he to disappoint the lad? Unfortunately, he wasn't the only one Billy invited.

Alma shoved the rest of the cookie into her mouth and sighed. "Billy, I thought you brought three poles."

"I only have two on account I thought just one of you would show up. Since you both did, you'll have to share."

She sighed, then looked at the pole. "You go ahead, Oliver. I'm too upset to fish."

He nodded his thanks and picked it up. After he cast his line, he glanced at her. "So why don't I speak with Hawthorne and find out a few things for you?"

She gasped. "You'd do that?"

"Why not?" He shrugged. "In all honesty, Alma, I don't think he's a threat to your business."

"What? How can you say that? Of course he is."

"Nah, he ain't," Billy said.

They stared at him and Oliver smiled. "What makes you say that?"

Billy, seated between them, glanced at one then the other. "On account he told Ma he was trying to only order things Alma had little, or not at all. He doesn't expect to carry the same things she does. But doesn't expect her not to carry any tools either." His face scrunched up. "Did that come out right?"

Oliver smiled. "There, you see? He means you no harm." He cast his line again.

Alma grabbed another cookie from Billy's lunch sack. "I still don't trust him. Who's to say he didn't tell your mother that just to throw me off? I can't let this go until I find out exactly what's going on."

"Then why don't you ask him?"

The three of them jumped. Oliver got to his feet, saw Etta Whitehead standing behind them, and relaxed. "Oh, it's you, Miss Whitehead. You gave us a fright."

"She didn't scare me." Billy cast his line again, took

another bite of his sandwich, and gave them each a proud smile.

Oliver tried not to laugh. "What brings you out here? I thought this was supposed to be a secret fishing spot." He eyed Billy, who grinned back.

"I think everyone in town knows this place." Miss Whitehead joined them on the grassy bank and sat next to Oliver. "I was taking a break, heard voices and came to see who was here."

"That's dangerous," he commented.

"How so?" She picked up a rock and threw it across the creek.

"Well, what if it wasn't us?" Oliver argued. "What if it was a gang of outlaws?"

Billy laughed. "That's silly, everyone knows outlaws don't fish."

Oliver and the women looked at the boy as if he'd just grown a third eye. "Billy," Oliver said. "Even outlaws have to eat."

Billy's face scrunched up. "But I heard outlaws are so busy outlawing that they don't have time to fish."

"But they might fish for food," Miss Whitehead said.

"Or come to the creek for a nap," Alma added. "Outlawing must be exhausting."

Oliver noted the strained look on the women's faces and figured he'd better change the subject. They were trying to keep the conversation light for Billy's sake, but any mention of outlaws caused more than a little angst in

Apple Blossom. "Well, there are no outlaws around here," he stated. "It's just the four of us now."

"Fishing!" Billy added with glee. He grinned at the rest of them, then cast his line again.

"Nothing happens when you're fishing," Alma said on a sigh.

Billy grinned again. "Except kissing." He gave Oliver a pointed look. "Ya better not kiss either of them, or you know what will happen."

Alma snorted. "What?"

Oliver became tight-lipped. Everyone knew Billy's philosophy about kissing at the fishing hole.

"You'll have to get married," the boy said. "Look what happened to Mr. Conrad and Sheriff Cassie!"

Even Miss Whitehead laughed. "I guess it's a good thing I don't fish much."

"Me neither," Alma added. She smiled at Oliver and left it at that.

He wasn't sure if he'd just been insulted or not. Oh, well, he'd keep quiet.

Miss Whitehead reached into her skirt pocket and pulled out an apple. The four sat in companionable silence, and Oliver found he enjoyed being here with some company. He smiled at Alma. "Here, you can fish for a while." He handed her the pole.

She took it, cast the line again, then munched her cookie.

He looked at the blue sky, what few white clouds there were, then the creek. This was a peaceful spot, beautiful and quiet. The sun was warm; the birds were singing, and he could spend the rest of the day here. He'd been so busy helping everyone with different building projects and whatnot, he hadn't taken a moment for himself. Well, until the whole skunk ordeal, but that was forced time off. Still, he hadn't thought to come here and enjoy the creek. Not like this.

He took a peek at the women. They both looked content at the moment. Even Alma. Good. He hoped she resolved her differences with Hawthorne soon or she'd make herself (and everyone else) miserable.

Soon Alma excused herself to go back to her store. She stood on the bank and stared at the creek a moment. "Is something wrong?" Oliver asked.

She shook her head. "No, just thinking. This is a good thinking spot."

"I agree," Miss Whitehead said. "I come here now and then and eat my lunch."

He looked at her discarded apple core. "That was lunch?"

"Dessert. I ate my sandwich on the way here." She picked up the core and tossed it into the bushes. "The deer will like that." She lay back, closed her eyes and sighed.

Billy's face screwed up. "How can you take a nap at a time like this? We're fishing."

She opened one eye. "You're fishing, and Mr. Darling is fishing. I'm closing my eyes and enjoying the sun on my face."

Billy rolled his eyes. "Fine, more fish for us."

"You haven't caught any," Alma pointed out as she headed for the trail.

"Would you like me to walk you back to town?" Oliver offered.

Alma stopped, looked at them, then at the trail leading into the woods. "Well, if you wouldn't mind."

He nodded. The incident that took the lives of the town posse happened just months ago, and everyone was still jittery. It was the only thing of that nature to happen in the town's history, and hopefully would never happen again. But it was on everyone's minds.

Oliver turned to Miss Whitehead and Billy. "I'm going to walk Alma back, then I'll return."

"What for?" Miss Whitehead asked, eyes still closed.

"So I can escort you and Billy back."

Etta sat up and looked at him but said nothing.

He joined Alma and off they went.

The trail wound through the woods, which were a mix of trees, brush, and grassy patches. It led to the small meadow where the town cemetery was, then the main road. Alma didn't say a word until they arrived at the latter. "Well, that was nice." She took in a lungful of air, then looked down the road that led into town. "Thanks for walking me back." She took another deep breath, as if to brace herself, and started walking.

"You'll be nice to Mr. Hawthorne, right?" He called after her.

She stopped and turned around. "So long as he's civil to me, yes."

Oliver sighed. He didn't believe her. "Do me a favor and let my brothers know where I am."

She nodded, turned and started down the road.

Oliver shook his head in dismay. He didn't know what was in Alma's head when it came to Hawthorne and wasn't sure if he wanted to find out. What he considered, however, was whether he wanted to spend more time in Apple Blossom before returning to England. He was liking it here. Perhaps too much.

Dora stared at Phileas as he ate his sandwich. Conrad was there, as were Sterling, Letty, Cassie, Flint and Lacey. Irving and Sarah were still at the future bakery, making a list of materials they'd need for the first floor. As soon as they were done, they'd join them. They sent Flint and Lacey ahead to get them fed. She had no idea where Jean and Wallis were.

"Where's Oliver?" Sterling asked.

"I don't have the foggiest," Phileas said. "He disappeared earlier, and I haven't seen him since."

"He's with Billy," Flint announced.

"Yeah," Lacey said. "We saw him. Alma and Billy walked by when we were sweeping the downstairs." She took another bite of sandwich then tried to feed some to her doll.

"He's with Alma?" Phileas said. "Where were they going?"

"Billy had his fishing poles with him," Flint said. "I asked if I could go too, but Ma said no."

"We had to come here and eat," Lacey added with a frown.

"Fishing?" Sterling said. At least he didn't sound annoyed.

"Well, why not?" Phileas stared at what remained of his sandwich. "I think we could all use a break."

Dora nodded. "You deserve one." She'd kept quiet until now, content to listen to the others talk. "I don't blame Oliver for going with Billy."

Phileas wiped his mouth with a napkin. "We have been working hard." He looked away, as if looking at her was somehow painful. Was he regretting having to work on the hotel?

"Things around here have been out of sorts since you arrived," she said. "We can't keep asking you to do things for us." Now she looked away. She didn't want any of the Darlings to leave. She'd grown quite fond of them, one in particular, and wasn't sure she could stand to see Phileas go. But he had to, and everyone knew it.

Sterling smiled at Letty, then looked at the others. "Dora's right. We've been trying so hard to get things done in a short time, and we're wearing ourselves out. Phileas, you should see about getting a message to Mother and Father."

He blanched. "What?"

"Sterling's right." Letty smiled at him. "Why not stay a while longer? That way you're not worn out by the time you leave."

Dora's heart pounded. If Phileas and Oliver stayed on, she was doomed. Unless... "How long would it take you to finish the hotel?"

"I couldn't say." He sat back in his chair. "It depends on how much you want done."

"And what about Irving and Sarah's new place?"

"There are enough of us to handle both," Sterling said. "So long as we have a little more time to get things done."

"And Mr. Hawthorne?" Dora asked. Why not throw him into the mix?

Conrad rolled his eyes. "Hawthorne. Phileas, you and Ollie shouldn't have to worry about him. We'll take care of it."

"And anything else that comes up," Sterling said. "But it would help if you could stay longer."

Dora glanced around the table. "How much longer?"

Phileas shrugged. "That's a good question."

Sterling studied the dining room, and Dora knew he was calculating the time it would take to finish the hotel. "Hmm, a month or more."

Phileas almost spewed lemonade on Flint. "Month or more?"

Dora sank a little in her chair. Month... she could fall madly in love with him by then. "I'd better fetch dessert." She rose from her chair and hurried to the kitchen. She was miserable enough now. But adding more than a few weeks to this torture, and she didn't know what she'd do.

Letty entered the kitchen. "Can I help?"

"It's just cookies." She went to the cookie jar, picked it up and handed it to her. "Take this."

Letty held it and started for the dining room. "Dora." She stopped and faced her. "Is there something wrong?"

She didn't bother turning around. "What makes you say that?"

There was a pause. "You don't seem yourself, that's all."

Her shoulders slumped. "It's the work. I've been busy for a while now, you know that."

"Yes, of course, that's it. Let me know if you need my help."

Dora listened to the kitchen door swing back and forth as Letty left. Unfortunately, the help she needed she could have used about a week ago. Maybe then she wouldn't be falling in love with Phileas.

Phileas tried not to gape at Sterling every time he looked at him. What was the man thinking? If he stayed on for a week, even two, he might hold out. But more than that and he was doomed! Sterling was supposed to help keep him from falling in love, not making it easier to.

Letty returned to the table with the cookie jar. Good.

Maybe a handful of cookies would help keep his mind off Dora. Though he doubted they would help much.

When the jar passed to him, he took a few then eyed Sterling. "Can I speak to you a moment?"

"Certainly." Sterling left his chair and motioned toward the lobby.

Phileas followed him outside to the boardwalk. "What are you doing?"

Sterling closed the hotel doors. "What do you mean?"

He gaped at him. "What we talked about." Phileas glanced at the doors. "I'm struggling, I admit it."

Sterling gave him a sage nod. "Hmm, well then, it's a good thing I told the others. Between the five of us, we'll keep you on the straight and narrow road to home."

"In a few weeks?"

"No." Sterling shook his head. "Definitely not."

Phileas couldn't believe it. Was he saying what he thought he was? "You were serious about a month?"

"No," Sterling admitted, "it could be longer."

Phileas gaped at him. "I don't have longer."

Sterling pulled him by the arm to the bench by the door and sat him down. "Yes, you do. If you don't have to worry about Dora, then think of all the work you can get done."

"What?"

"We'll keep her busy. She can help Sarah while we work on the hotel. Then Sarah can help her with some things in the hotel while we help Irving with the bigger things."

Phileas raised an eyebrow. "What about Hawthorne?"

Sterling waved at the air. "We'll get to him, eventually. The point is, if we work things this way, then you can stay with us a while longer, and not fall in love."

Okay, so it made sense. "So where's the nearest telegraph office?"

"Virginia City. The captain and Mr. Featherstone should be back soon. You can speak to the captain then. Tell him we don't mind paying him to take our message to Virginia City and have it sent."

Phileas nodded slowly. "So a month could turn into two."

"If you want. Who says Mother or Father need a set date just so they can meet you at the train station when you return? The two of you could just as easily take a coach home."

He gasped. "Mother will go quite mad."

Sterling laughed. "Most likely."

Phileas frowned. "Yes, and Oliver and I will have to deal with her. Great."

"I'll send a letter with you to… soften the blow, shall we say?"

Phileas left the bench. "You want two extra hands for a time, is that it?"

Sterling slowly got to his feet. "No, brother. None of us are ready to let you two go."

He stared at him a moment. "And you'll help me to... you know."

"Not fall in love?" Sterling slapped him on the back. "We'll do our best."

Phileas sighed. "Very well, then. I'll speak to the captain tomorrow." He looked Sterling in the eyes. "Mother will be furious."

"Probably, but after being free from the constraints of our social obligations and class restrictions, I'm much less sympathetic to her plight. She wanted us married, and four of us are giving her what she wants." Sterling grinned and went inside.

Phileas stood, his chest tight. "What about what I want?"

Chapter Sixteen

After lunch, Dora went for a walk. She wanted to be alone to think, feel, and try to figure out how she was going to cope with life once Phileas and Oliver were gone. For one, her friends were marrying the remaining Darlings, and two, that meant she'd be quite alone.

Now she understood what Jean went through. She was afraid of being left behind, watching her friends get further and further away. There was an empty feeling, knowing Phileas would be gone soon.

She walked up the boardwalk toward the bank and wondered if Agnes would pop out as she passed. But she doubted it. Agnes had been unusually quiet since Mr. Featherstone went fishing with the captain, and she wasn't looking forward to whatever had kept her occupied all this time. For all anyone knew, Agnes was starting a town paper and gossiping about all of them in it. What a horrible thought! Either that or she was getting a good dose of what it was like to have a little time to herself. Maybe she liked it.

Dora walked past the bank, then turned and headed toward the sheriff's office. Beyond that she could walk to the cemetery or follow the trail to the creek and Billy's fishing hole. It was supposed to be a secret, but of course almost everyone in town knew where it was.

She strolled past the sheriff's office but there was no sign of Cassie or Conrad. Maybe they were making rounds. When she reached the cemetery, she stopped and stared at the gravestones. A chill went up her spine as she strolled to her father's grave. "Hello, Pa." She knelt down and plucked a few blades of grass. Someone had mowed the area and folks had brought flowers to their loved ones.

Dora sighed and took in her father's bare grave. She would have to pick some flowers and bring them. It had been a while. A long while. "I'm sorry I haven't come by. I've been... busy." She wiped a tear from her eye. "But I wanted to talk to you about something. I did a stupid thing, and I don't know what to do about it now."

She sighed and leaned to one side, bracing herself with a hand. "I think I'm in love." She laughed weakly. "Yeah, I know, it's silly. Me in love? Did you ever think it would happen? I didn't." She sniffed back a tear and hoped she didn't start crying. She grieved like everyone else after the incident, but sometimes it hit, and she cried and couldn't stop. "I miss you, Pa. I wish you were here.

The problem is, I think my heart is lost. If he takes it with him, then what do I do? I can't follow. I must stay here."

A breeze rustled the leaves in the surrounding trees. Dora sniffed back more tears and wiped her eyes. "I'm sorry, Pa. I have to go. I can't do this." She climbed to her feet, brushed off her skirt and turned back. But instead of heading back to town, she started down the trail to Billy's fishing hole.

She hadn't gone far when she heard voices – Oliver and Etta's. "Dora," Etta said as they came around a bend in the trail. "What are you doing here?"

Dora noted their bright faces. Were they having a good conversation, or just enjoying each other's company? "Oh, nothing. Taking a walk."

"Billy and his father are fishing," Oliver said. "Mr. Watson came to fetch Billy and wound up fishing with him instead." He pointed down the trail. "You could join them or walk with us. I'm escorting Etta back to town."

"That's kind of you." Though they weren't far from town, one reason folks didn't go to Billy's fishing spot often was because it was remote, and no one wanted to be caught unawares by a stranger. Any stranger. "I can walk with you."

"Jolly good," Oliver said. "The more the merrier, as they say."

She smiled. "We missed you at lunch."

"I know, but Billy can be very persuasive."

"That he can be," Etta laughed.

Dora studied them. "No wonder you look happy. You were having fun."

"Billy had the most fun," Oliver said. "That boy is either going to be a politician or... well, I'm not sure what else. He has a way about him, you know?"

Dora couldn't help but giggle. "The whole town knows."

The three walked in silence for a time before they reached town. The day was peaceful and warm, and Dora forgot what an enjoyable walk could do for her. She ought to walk every day if she was able. But she'd been so busy since the Darlings came, she hadn't had time.

When they got back to town, Agnes was standing on the boardwalk in front of the bank speaking with Mr. Miller, her bank teller. She took one look at the three of them and scowled. "What are you three doing? Etta, why aren't you minding the livery stable? And you," she snapped at Dora. "Don't you have wallpaper to hang?"

She stiffened. "I'm taking a break, if you don't mind. By the way, the lobby is spectacular."

"That may be, but you won't get all the work out of that man you want. I can tell you that."

Dora didn't comment and kept walking. Thank goodness Captain Stanley would be back today. Agnes seemed crankier than normal with Mr. Featherstone gone.

They parted ways at the hotel. Etta retreated across the street to the livery stable, and Oliver returned to do a little more fishing with Billy and his father. She smiled.

His escorting Etta back was a gentlemanly thing to do. Speaking of gentlemen, she wondered if Phileas was back at work.

When she went inside, there was no one in the lobby. Dora glanced at the dining room, saw no one there and headed for the kitchen. It too was empty. She sighed and sat at the kitchen table. There were a few small chores she wanted to get done before she thought about dinner.

She left the kitchen for her quarters, did some dusting and straightening, cleaned her bathroom, then did some mending. Not once did she hear Phileas or anyone else for that matter. Where was everyone? No matter, she'd go about her business and not worry who was in the hotel right now.

Funny thing, she missed the noise and commotion of having a full house. She missed Phileas.

In the kitchen, she made herself some tea, then leafed through a cookbook she had, looking for something new to make. She found a recipe for stuffed roast chicken and got to work.

Dora hadn't been working long when Phileas strolled into the kitchen. "Good afternoon," he greeted her. "You didn't happen to run across Oliver while you were out, did you?"

She stared at him a moment, her throat thick with emotion. She missed her father something awful, but the thought of this man leaving Apple Blossom almost tore her heart out. "Y-yes, I did." She turned away. "He's still fishing with Billy." She went to the icebox, took out some carrots and set them on the worktable.

"Is there anything else?"

She slowly raised her head to him. "No."

He stood on the other side of the worktable, reached across it, and tucked a finger under her chin. "Are you sure?"

She swallowed hard and nodded.

He studied her a moment. "Right, then. I'm off to fetch my brother." His eyes lingered on her a second or two, then he left.

As soon as he was gone, Dora let out the breath she was holding and leaned on the table. That had to be the most intimate moment of her life. And all he did was put a finger to her chin! Merciful heavens, what would happen if he kissed her?

Phileas marched out of the hotel, down the street and straight to the trail to the fishing hole. At the moment, he'd like Oliver's head on a platter, but would settle for giving him a good talking-to instead. Why was he still fishing with Billy? He was supposed to be keeping him from doing things like what he just did in the kitchen! Great Scott, what if he'd kissed her? Oh, the agony of it all! And what about Sterling? He'd gone round the bend as the locals say. He had to be insane to want him and

Oliver to stay. Good grief, he might blurt out a proposal over fried chicken one night and then what?

"It's not possible that she..." He stopped in the middle of the trail and stared straight ahead. "Oh, dear me. She looked like..." He didn't dare say it aloud. But he swore Dora was looking at him with longing in her eyes. No, that was impossible. He took a breath, straightened his jacket, then continued down the trail. He had to be seeing things. The look on her face was shock that he would make such an intimate gesture. What was he thinking anyway?

He stopped again, rapped his head with his fist a few times, then continued. "Idiot, what *were* you thinking?"

He walked along the trail and realized he hadn't been down this way before. When he stopped this time, he admired his surroundings for a few moments. "Oh, will you look at all this?" He turned a full circle to take everything in. "It's beautiful."

"We like to think so."

He spun to the voice. Mr. Watson stood in the middle of the trail, Oliver and Billy right behind him. "Hello. I was just coming to fetch Ollie."

His brother waved at him. "Sorry, Phileas. Time got away from me."

"Indeed, it did. Next time, do let me know where you're running off to." He straightened his jacket again and squared his shoulders.

Oliver made his way around Billy's father. "Did you start without me?"

"No, but I was about to. We need to start stripping wallpaper in the dining room."

"Yes, of course. Forgive me." Oliver looked sheepish as he scurried down the trail. Billy chased after him.

Phileas sighed, then offered Mr. Watson a smile. "After you." He motioned to the trail.

He gave him a curt nod and passed him. With a sigh, Phileas followed.

When they reached town, Billy and his father headed for the livery stable, Oliver for the hotel. Phileas hesitated when he heard some noise coming from behind the saloon. Was the captain back? He decided to investigate and strolled that way.

When he went around to the rear of the building, he spied the captain, Mr. Featherstone, and a wiry elderly man. He was short with wispy white hair and wore a thick pair of spectacles that made his blue eyes look huge. He stood clutching a worn carpetbag to his chest as the captain unloaded the wagon. "Need any help?" Phileas offered.

Captain Stanley grinned ear to ear. "Phileas, lad. Meet McSweeny!" He slapped the little man on the back and almost sent him sprawling. He coughed and sputtered a few times as he righted himself, then shoved his spectacles up his nose.

Phileas' face screwed up. "McSweeny...you mean, Captain Charles McSweeny? The man you served as cabin boy?" He smiled. "Conrad told me all about that."

Mr. McSweeny squinted at him. "Charles was my older brother."

Captain Stanley slapped him again and the little man pitched forward. This time Phileas caught him. "That's right," the captain said. "This here is Vernon, Captain McSweeny's little brother and ship's cook! Guess what he'll be doing in town?"

Phileas took in the little man's squinting face and cringed. "I can scarce imagine."

Captain Stanley put an arm around Mr. McSweeny and crushed him to his side. "He's going to cook, of course. I thought he could cook in the saloon to start and if he wants to open his own place in town later, he can."

Phileas studied the pair. The captain towered over the little man, and it was all he could do not to laugh at the sight. "Cook, you say?" He took a good look at Mr. McSweeny. He was squinting something awful as he tried to take in his surroundings. "Oh, my ..."

Captain Stanley laughed and rubbed one meaty hand up and down one of Mr. McSweeny's arms, lifting him off his feet with each upward stroke. The man couldn't weigh over ninety pounds soaking wet.

"Well," Phileas said cheerfully. "Welcome to Apple Blossom." He searched for Mr. Featherstone, but he'd already disappeared. "I say, where did your fishing partner go?"

The captain let Mr. McSweeny go and waved a dismissive hand. "Ah, he's worried his sea hag of a wife will be upset we took longer than expected. But I had to

197

give McSweeny time to decide if he wanted to come here, and of course gather his things."

"Is that so?"

Mr. McSweeny squinted at him with a weak smile. "Imagine my surprise when the captain walked into the hotel."

"Vernon was the new cook there," Captain Stanley said. "But not anymore! I convinced him Apple Blossom was the place to be."

Phileas bit his lower lip to keep from laughing. "I see. My, my." He turned around, shut his eyes tight a moment, then faced them again. Poor McSweeny looked like he'd blow away in a strong wind. And he could cook? "So, tell me, sir. Do you have a special dish you're known for?"

"Special!" Captain Stanley barked. He slapped poor McSweeny on the back again. "Why, Vernon McSweeny was one of the best ship's cooks around. He can whip up anything you want!"

Phileas' eyebrows shot up. "Anything?"

"Sure!" He smiled at the little man. "Can't you, McSweeny?"

McSweeny squinted at him. "Oh, yes, anything."

Phileas' eyebrows rose further. "Hmm, what about plum pudding?"

McSweeny's lip curled upward as he squinted at him. "Oh, yes. Not a problem."

He blinked, a hand to his chest. "What about trifle? Mincemeat pie?"

McSweeny didn't blink an eye. Probably because he was squinting so hard. "Yes, yes, those are easy."

Phileas' jaw dropped as he looked at the captain. He stood proudly, a knowing look on his face. "I know what you're thinking," Captain Stanley said. "How can a pipsqueak like McSweeny make all that?" The captain winked. "He's been all around the world, he has!"

Phileas smiled in delight. "I bet you have some tales to tell."

McSweeny smiled. "Yes, a few." He nodded to himself, then looked at the saloon. "Where's your place, Stan?"

Captain Stanley smiled, pointed his friend in the right direction, and gave him a little shove. "Just keep walking until you bump into the building."

Phileas openly gawked as McSweeny slowly shuffled his way forward. "Is he going to be all right?"

"Of course. He might be blind as a bat, but he can manage. You watch, he won't fall over when he reaches the back porch."

Phileas continued to watch McSweeny head toward the back of the saloon. "Are you sure about that?"

The captain held up a hand. "Just watch."

Sure enough, when McSweeny got within a few feet of the building, he stopped. "Amazing," Phileas commented. Also amazing was the fact he hadn't thought of Dora once while speaking to the captain and McSweeny. Maybe the old cook was just the distraction he needed right now.

Chapter Seventeen

N ews of Apple Blossom's latest arrival spread fast. Dora hadn't so much as put her chicken in the oven when Agnes came marching into the kitchen. "Did you hear?"

She sighed. "Francis and the captain are back?"

"That's Mr. Featherstone to you, and yes, they're back. But that's not all. Captain Stanley has brought another stranger to town!"

That got her attention. "What? Who?"

Agnes put her hands on her hips. "One Vernon McSweeny, or so I'm told. Francis never was one for digging for information. But rest assured, I'll find out all there is to know about him!" She paced from one side of the kitchen to the other. "He's supposed to be some skilled cook. Ha! Have you seen him yet?"

Dora stared at her in stunned silence for a moment.

"No." She was so taken by surprise that she forgot what she wanted to do next. "Who is this again?"

Agnes rolled her eyes. "Why do I waste my time?" She turned on her heel and headed for the nearest door. "The lobby looks wonderful, by the way." With that, she disappeared into the hall.

Dora stared after her, jaw slack. "Thank you." She shook her head, took a breath, then went about her business. Goodness gracious, what next?

She got her answer soon enough. "Dora!" Phileas called from down the hall. "Did you hear the news?" He burst through the kitchen door from the dining room. "We have a new resident!"

She couldn't help but smile at the delight on his face. "So I hear. Didn't you see Agnes?"

"Yes, she was in the lobby looking envious." He grinned. "But I didn't think she'd shower me with accolades of praise, so I came straight here."

"What's this man's name again?"

He caught his breath. "Vernon McSweeny. He's a cook the captain knew back in the day. And he's the brother of one Charles McSweeny, the captain our captain served as cabin boy to." He leaned against the worktable.

She noticed his disheveled look. "Did you run here?"

He smiled and shook his head. "A gentleman does not run; he walks very quickly."

The look suited him, and she tried to turn away but

couldn't. He was so incredibly handsome; she didn't know what to do with herself in that moment. "*Can* he cook?"

"He says he can." Phileas went to the hutch, took a glass and headed out the door to the pump.

She waited for him to return, then took a pitcher from a cupboard and handed it to him. "Do you mind?"

He looked into her eyes and smiled. "Not at all." He drained the glass he'd filled, then went out the door again.

Dora watched him out the back door window, her heart in her throat. She'd never seen him so excited before. This McSweeny must be quite the cook to have Phileas so elated.

When he returned, he set the pitcher on the work-table. "What's in the oven?"

She smiled. "You're in a good mood."

"Yes, I suppose I am. It's not every day you meet someone in a place like this who can make trifle." He gave her a hopeful look. "You wouldn't happen to…"

"No, can't say that I have. But if you could get me a recipe, I could try." She looked into his eyes. "Is it your favorite?"

He laughed. "One of many. I should find Oliver and get to work on the dining room."

She nodded, unsure of what to say. If she kept talking to him, it would only make her more heartsick. She settled for a smile instead.

His eyes roamed her face a moment before he smiled

and, to her surprise, kissed her on the cheek and hurried from the room.

Dora stood, her hand to her cheek, and gaped at the door. What just happened? Did he really just kiss her? "Oh, my, oh, dear!" She glanced at the oven, then the door leading to the hall, and headed straight for it. "Alma." Indeed, she was the only person close enough at the moment to talk some sense into her.

Dora hurried through the lobby and out the door. She didn't stop, didn't look back, and broke into a run in the middle of the street.

When she rushed into the general store, Alma spun around to face her. "Goodness, you scared me!" She fanned herself with a hand a moment. "What did you need?"

Dora ran to the counter. "Oh, Alma! Don't let me do it!"

Alma's face screwed up. "Do what?"

"Fall in love!" She folded her arms on the counter and let her head fall onto them. "I'm in so much trouble!"

"What did you do?" Alma asked with concern.

Dora looked at her. "I'm falling in love with a Darling!"

Alma's eyes rounded to saucers. "Which one? Goodness, I hope it's not one that's already taken."

"Of course not." Dora straightened. "It's Phileas."

Alma sighed. "Oh, that one." She shook her head in dismay. "I'm afraid you might be done for."

"What?!"

Alma shrugged. "Well, face it, the two of you are perfect for one another. You both have impeccable taste, at least in my opinion. You like to entertain, and he seems to like it too. Let's see, what else?" She bit her lip and shut one eye. "And you both love the hotel."

Dora sagged against the counter. "Did you have to say all of that?" She sighed and shook her head. "I'm doomed to heartache."

Alma's eyes widened. "Dora, I can't help you."

Dora rubbed her eyes with the backs of her hands. "Why not?"

Alma gave her a heartfelt smile. "Isn't it obvious? You're already in love with him."

Dora stared at her a moment, then put the back of her hand against her forehead with a groan. "No, I'm not." She realized what she was doing and let her hand drop—she probably looked like some character in a melodrama. "I'm sorry. I can't think straight."

"No one in love can."

She groaned again. "Letty was supposed to keep me from doing this." She smacked the counter, then made a face. "Ow."

Alma took her hands in hers. "Have you spoken to Phileas yet?"

"No, of course not. He has no interest in me." She fought the urge to pull her hands away.

"Dora, even with Letty and I helping, I think you'd suffer the same outcome."

Dora sank against the counter. "What am I going to do? He might stay longer than planned to finish the hotel and help his brothers. If he does that, I'm not sure I can take it."

Alma let go of her hands. "I'm sorry, but I don't know what I can say to help you."

Dora nodded in understanding. "Thank you anyway." She turned and trudged to the doors. Once outside she looked across the street at the saloon. "Captain Stanley, of course." She smiled and hurried across the street.

When she entered the saloon, the captain and a thin white-haired man were at the bar. Captain Stanley smiled and waved at her. "Dora, come join us."

She smiled and crossed the saloon to the bar. "Hello." Her eyes fixed on the newcomer. He wore thick-lensed spectacles that made his eyes appear larger than they were, making it hard not to stare. "You're Captain Stanley's friend?"

He squinted at her. "Yes."

"This here's Vernon McSweeny—not to be confused with my horse," the captain said. "I guess I'd better call him Vernon from now on."

She offered the man her hand. "Pleased to meet you. I'm Dora Jones. I run the hotel." She clasped her hands together. "I hear you're a cook?"

"That's right," Mr. McSweeny said.

"Have you come to town to start a restaurant?"

"Don't know yet," the little man said. "I have to see if I like it here."

She smiled. "Well, I have an idea. If it's agreeable with you, would you like to do some cooking at the hotel? I have a lot of people staying there and it would give you a chance to try your cooking out on a few folks."

He rubbed his chin a few times. "Hmm, what do you think, Stan?"

"Will he get paid?" the captain asked.

"No, their meals are included in their room cost."

Captain Stanley paced a few times. "Vernon, you ought to do it. Give them a good taste, then if they want more, they'll have to come here to get more." He smacked him on the back. "Then you can charge them!"

Mr. McSweeny smiled. "That's good thinking, Stan." He smiled and Dora noticed he had dimples.

"Then you'll do it?" she asked.

"I will." Mr. McSweeny offered Dora his hand and she shook it. Now she could breathe easy. All she had to do was come up with an excuse not to be around at dinnertime. One less meal to spend with Phileas.

Phileas watched everyone at the table. They had a guest tonight, and he wondered what the captain and his cohort McSweeny were doing there. Maybe Dora was just being neighborly and invited them.

"Fine as always," the captain said as he stabbed at his chicken. "Right, McSweeny?"

The wiry little man sniffed at the chicken on his plate. He hadn't taken a bite yet. Dora looked like she'd just been put on trial for murder, and he was the judge.

He cut another small piece, sniffed at it, then popped it in his mouth. "Hmm, not bad. Could use a bit more rosemary." He smiled at her, and Phileas thought she was going to fall out of her chair. What was wrong with her this evening?

"I'm glad you like it," she finally said. "It's new."

Mr. McSweeny studied each of Phileas' brothers, including him. "What part of England are you from?"

Phileas noted the man had a slight accent. "Sussex."

"Ah, I know a duke there. Met him and his duchess during one of my many travels. They had a wonderful cook."

Sterling and Irving exchanged a look, as did the rest of them. "We live near the Duke of Stantham."

"That's the one." He took another bite of chicken. "Hmm, a pinch of paprika would do nicely as well."

Dora forced a smile, nodded, then took another bite of her food.

Phileas was intrigued. "Mr. McSweeny, how do you know the Duke of Stantham?"

Mr. McSweeny cut up more of his chicken. "Met him in London. We got to talking, and wound up discussing pot roast."

Phileas and his brothers exchanged another look. "Pot roast?" he said. "Well, that's an interesting subject."

"Turned out it was. He went on and on about this great recipe he had and before I knew it, I was going home with him and the duchess to prove to him it couldn't possibly be the best."

Conrad laughed. "You went home with him to try it?"

Mr. McSweeny smiled. "That's right." He took another bite of chicken, then poked a potato. "But not before making one of my own. His cook didn't like that." He got back to eating, ignoring their shocked looks.

Phileas leaned toward Wallis. "Do you remember hearing anything about this?"

"Nothing," he said in a low voice. "But then, having a ship's cook make a roast for His Grace wouldn't be too outlandish. Not at the Stantham estate."

"Quite right," Phileas agreed. He stole a glance at Dora. She kept eyeing McSweeny like he would sprout wings and fly away. Was she afraid he'd leave without telling her what he really thought of her cooking?

He tried to concentrate on his food and hoped she baked a pie for dessert. He smelled something baking earlier but wasn't sure if she baked it or if Jean brought something over. Sterling, Wallis and Oliver kept him occupied all afternoon. True to their word, his brothers were doing their best to keep him from falling in love.

Unfortunately, when he gave Dora that peck on the cheek earlier, it got the better of him. Thank goodness she left the hotel. He didn't even care where she went so long as she was gone for a time. He had the silly notion of getting down on one knee after kissing her creamy cheek. What a disaster that would have been. For one, he still wasn't sure she had any feelings for him whatsoever.

"I bet McSweeny here can whip up all kinds of things," Dora blurted. "When should he start?"

Irving dropped his fork. "Start? What do you mean?"

Dora went bright red. "Well, after speaking with the captain regarding Mr. McSweeny's culinary talents. I thought it would be nice to let him have the chance to cook for all of you." She took a quick bite of her chicken. Did she think no one would like the idea?

Phileas smiled. "I think that would be fine. Especially since Mr. McSweeny knows how to make trifle."

Oliver gasped in delight. "He does?"

"I do," McSweeny confirmed, then got back to eating.

Oliver looked at everyone around the table like he'd just been given a huge Christmas present. "Trifle."

"And plum pudding," Phileas added.

Conrad gasped, then coughed. "What's that you say?"

"McSweeny can make all sorts of things." The captain slapped poor McSweeny on the back, almost making him choke. He coughed and sputtered and tried to catch his breath.

"I say," Irving said. "Is he all right?"

"He'll be fine," Captain Stanley assured. "Won't you McSweeny?" He made to slap him again.

The little man held up a hand to stop him. "Let's leave it at that, Stan." He took a sip of water, face red, then smiled at Dora. "Are you sure you don't mind me taking over your kitchen?"

"Not at all." She smiled nervously. "Everyone's looking forward to trying your cooking." She glanced around the table again. "Right?"

"Oh, yes, of course," Phileas said. Hmm, why did she look so nervous? Was she worried he was a horrible cook? Only one way to find out.

The conversation changed to Hawthorne and his hardware store. Once again, he was working late and didn't show up for a meal. Dora had already set a plate aside for him in the warming oven. Hawthorne had better hope Oliver didn't get to it first. If he returned to the hotel too late, it might be gone.

Phileas listened to the different snippets of conversation and tried not to look at Dora. She was quiet, and he thought of speaking to her after dinner, but that would be a mistake. Besides, Sterling and the others wouldn't let him. He was supposed to be staying away from her. Otherwise, what was the point of helping him? He could hear his brothers complaining now.

Phileas finished his meal, then discussed the rooms upstairs with Oliver and Wallis. As soon as the dining room was finished, they'd begin the guest rooms. He also had to figure out what to write in his message to Mother and Father. He'd have to speak to the captain after dessert. Maybe he could walk back to the saloon with him and do it then. For some reason, he didn't want to let Dora know he was staying on for longer. Of course, if Sterling had his way, he'd be staying another couple of months, and he couldn't afford to. If he did, he'd lose his heart for sure.

Chapter Eighteen

Dora watched Phileas leave with the captain and Mr. McSweeny. Why he wanted to talk to him she didn't know and wasn't sure she wanted to. Besides, she was supposed to be staying away from him.

She started the dishes and tried not to think about him. It was all she could do to stay away from him just after dinner.

When the dishes were done, she retreated to the lobby to do some mending. She could do it in her own little parlor, but where was the fun in that? What if someone needed something?

So she sat and... waited, yes, that's what she was doing. She was waiting for...

"Dora," Sarah said as she came into the lobby. "What are you doing here?"

Dora started and almost fell off the sofa. "Oh, um, nothing."

Sarah crossed her arms and gave her a hard stare. "Mending in the lobby?" She glanced at the front windows and back. "You aren't waiting for Phileas to return, are you?"

"What, me? No. Why would I be waiting for him?"

"I'm not sure, considering you're trying to stay away from him. Sitting out here will not accomplish that." She let her arms drop and came to the sofa. "Come on, let's go."

Dora opened her mouth to speak, thought better of it, and got to her feet. "Fine, I'll sequester myself in my rooms."

"See that you do." Sarah headed for the stairs. "If you're serious about guarding your heart, then I suggest you do it." She gave her a pointed look before going up the stairs.

Dora stared at the floor a moment. Sarah was right, of course. If she wanted to stay away from Phileas, then she'd better do it.

She went down the hall to her rooms and stopped at the door. Her heart wanted to wait for him to come back to the hotel. In fact, shouldn't he have been back by now? What could keep him? Were he and the captain having some deep conversation? Was the captain helping him plan how to get everything done quicker so he could leave for England sooner? With her luck, that's exactly what was going on. And why should she argue? Isn't that what she wanted in the first place?

With a sigh, Dora went inside and sank onto her sofa. If she were smart, she'd have Phileas work on her living quarters. But no, it was best she spent as little time with him as possible. Problem was, she was already in love.

"I can't believe you know how to play whist," Phileas exclaimed happily.

Mr. McSweeny finished dealing the cards. He was partnered with Oliver while the captain was Phileas' partner. They'd been playing for two hours, with no end in sight. None of them had played for a time and were too engrossed in the game to stop.

"I've always enjoyed playing this," Captain Stanley said. "Was Captain McSweeny that taught me."

"He taught me too," the younger McSweeny said. "Charles was an excellent player."

The captain smiled. "That he was." He smiled at Phileas. "Now, what is it you wanted to ask me? We got to playing, and I forgot all about it."

"Oh, yes." Phileas cleared his throat. "I, um, wanted to know if you'd take a message to Virginia City the next time you go and see it sent." He glanced at Oliver and back. "We need to send a telegraph message to our parents."

The captain arched one bushy eyebrow. "Anything wrong?"

"No, just need to get a message to them."

Oliver leaned his way. "How long?"

He shrugged. "Sterling wants at least a month."

Oliver winced. "Mother will be furious."

"Don't I know it." He sighed and picked up his cards.

"Staying on a while longer, eh?" the captain said. "Well, there's nothing wrong with that. We're glad to have the two of you here. Gives McSweeny a couple extra bellies to fill. You'll give him your honest opinion on his cooking, right?"

"Of course." Oliver smiled at the little man. "I'll be the first to tell you what I think."

McSweeny smiled back and looked at his cards. "Fine, now let's play."

Phileas had been enjoying the game, but the thought of going home to face what was worse than a firing squad didn't sit well. Even worse, his heart wasn't in it like it was a few days ago. As soon as he and Oliver had finished the lobby, he'd started imagining what it would be like if he stayed. But there was a problem with that too. A big one.

By the time they finished another game, it was almost midnight. "Great Scott, look at the time." Phileas put his watch back in his pocket. "We must be going. Tell me, Mr. McSweeny, do you play chess?"

He squinted at him. It was amazing he could even see the cards. "I do."

"We'll inform Sterling. He loves the game, but he's been so busy with Letty and her place, he has had little chance to play."

"Doesn't Mr. Featherstone play too?" Oliver asked.

Captain Stanley gathered the cards. "He does. Your brother can get some good games in with any of us."

"You play too?" Oliver said.

"That I do, lad." He smiled at them. "I'll be heading to Virginia City in a few days. Have your message ready by then."

Phileas and Oliver said goodnight, then headed back to the hotel. "That was fun," Oliver commented. "We should do that again soon."

"I'm afraid it will have to wait until the captain returns from his next trip to Virginia City."

Oliver took him by the arm. "What are you going to say in the message?"

"Oliver..." Phileas stopped.

"What?"

"I don't think I can stay. I know I told Sterling I'd be open to it, but being here is getting harder by the day."

"Dora?"

He nodded. "If I can avoid her until we leave, it might not be so bad."

Oliver nodded. "I understand. I'll help you however I can. Just tell me what to do."

Phileas exhaled. "Thank you, Oliver. I appreciate it."

They walked in silence for a moment before Oliver spoke again. "Do you remember when we were kids, and we used to sneak into the duke's woods to play chess?"

Phileas chuckled. "Of course, I do. Sterling could never beat us back then. Not until he took a genuine interest in the game. Until he met Letty, it was all he thought about."

"I have a confession to make," Oliver said sheepishly. "I cheated."

Phileas stopped in his tracks, surprised. "You what?"

"On our last game with Sterling, when you went to the kitchen to sneak some biscuits from cook, I made a move while he wasn't looking."

Phileas couldn't help but laugh. "Oliver, that was years ago."

"I know, but I've been carrying it with me ever since." Oliver shrugged. "I'm sorry."

Phileas shook his head. "Don't worry about it. It's in the past."

They reached the hotel, Phileas bid Oliver goodnight before heading to his room. As he lay in bed, he couldn't shake off the dread that had lingered inside him for days. He didn't want to deal with their mother's constant nagging and belittling. Not to mention the thought of leaving his brothers behind made him feel empty. And the only thing that could fill that emptiness was sleeping downstairs.

He closed his eyes and tried to push the thoughts away, but they resurfaced even stronger. He needed to decide, and soon. How long should he stay? The longer he did, the worse he was going to feel. His heart ached now, and whereas he could distract himself with work, not even that could make him forget the pain was there. The only thing to do was keep avoiding Dora. But that hadn't been working well either. He couldn't stay away from her. The only other thing he could think to do was enlist more help. But who should he ask?

Too tired to think on it further, Phileas closed his eyes and let sleep overtake him. At least staying up late made it harder to lament that he'd fallen in love.

The next morning, Dora walked into the kitchen and stopped short. "Mr. McSweeny, what are you doing here?"

He picked up the coffeepot. "Want some?"

She stared at him bug-eyed. "Er, sure, but what are you doing here?"

He picked up a cup and saucer from the worktable and poured her a cup. "I'm making breakfast." He shoved the cup and saucer toward her.

She stood on the other side of the table, slack jawed. "I thought you'd make dinner tonight. No one said anything about breakfast."

"Stan said you wouldn't mind." He returned his attention to the stove and stirred some potatoes that were frying in a pan. She was so surprised at seeing him, she didn't notice he'd already started cooking.

"Well, I don't, but..." She peered into the pan. "My, those look good."

"Sit, have your coffee."

She studied him a moment. He squinted at everything! How good was his eyesight, anyway? "Er, fine." She went to the kitchen table and sat. "I don't suppose you're planning on making lunch too."

"Of course. How else can I test my cooking out? Your hotel guests are the perfect way to see what dishes will work when I start cooking at Stan's place."

"The saloon?"

"Yes, we discussed this last night. Weren't you listening?" He turned his potatoes then started cracking eggs into a pan.

Dora sat, unable to think. When did they discuss his making meals at the saloon? Just how befuddled was she?

She took a sip of coffee and tried to think but nothing came to mind. If she were smart, she'd take advantage of his offer. She could eat and run. What better way to stay away from Phileas? While he worked on the dining room, she could visit with Alma or walk to Sarah's house, take a look, then go to Letty's. If she timed things right, she could avoid Phileas for most of the day until he left.

She smiled at the thought and sipped more coffee.

It wasn't long before the Darlings filed into the kitchen. Mr. McSweeny shooed them right back out.

"Guests don't belong in the kitchen!" He waved a spatula at them and chased them into the dining room. "Sit. I'll bring the pot." He stomped back to the stove, brushing past her as he went.

She tried not to laugh then joined the others at the usual table, which she noticed had already been set. "Oh, my."

"What is he doing?" Wallis asked. "Why aren't you making breakfast?"

She gave everyone a helpless shrug. "He was cooking when I came into the kitchen. Speaking of which, who didn't lock the door last night?"

Oliver sank a little in his chair. "I'm afraid it was me. It was late when Phileas and I returned from the saloon."

Sterling frowned. "How late?"

She stole a glance at Phileas, who smiled at the others. "It was after midnight."

"What?" Conrad laughed. "What were you two doing at the saloon that late? Don't tell me you were drinking."

"Of course not," Phileas said. "We were playing whist."

Irving smiled. "Whist, you say?"

Phileas nodded. "Yes. Seems Mr. McSweeny learned it while he spent time in England."

Before anyone could say another word, Mr. Hawthorne entered the dining room and joined them. "Sorry I'm late." He looked around the table. "Is there still coffee in the pot?"

The Darlings exchanged the same mischievous look. Oh no, they wouldn't.

"Of course." Conrad grinned. "Help yourself."

Dora raised her eyebrows at him. Hawthorne was already on his way to the kitchen. "Sometimes I wonder about you all," she breathed.

She looked at the kitchen door as it swung back and forth a few times, then Hawthorne as he came running out, McSweeny hot on his heels. "Stay out of the kitchen! How can I cook when you keep interrupting me?" He gave them all a squinty-eyed frown and marched back inside.

Hawthorne gulped. "Who is that?"

"Oh, yes," Sterling said. "You and Mr. McSweeny haven't been properly introduced. He's cooking for us. For how long, we don't know. I believe that's up to Dora."

She straightened at the sound of her name. She'd been staring at Phileas and didn't realize it. "What?"

Oliver picked up his cup and looked at everyone over the rim, his eyes settling on Phileas.

Everyone else was staring at her. "Oh, well, I suppose he can cook until we get tired of him."

"But what if he's a really superb cook?" Wallis asked.

She blew out a breath. "Come now, he can't be *that* good."

Phileas took another bite of eggs. They were some of the best he'd ever had. "Superb."

"Does anyone mind if I take a couple of muffins with me?" Mr. Hawthorne asked. "I might work through lunch."

"I suggest you don't," Conrad said. "We might leave nothing for you, not if lunch is as good as this was."

Phileas noticed Dora staring at her empty plate. Like the rest of them, she'd eaten every bite. "What do you think?" He shouldn't start a conversation with her, but he was curious.

She looked around the table. "It was good, very good. I could get used to this." She set her napkin on the table and began to gather the dishes.

Phileas watched. He normally helped, but with McSweeny here, he could get to work on the dining room right away. He smiled at Oliver. "Ready?"

She seemed to take the hint that he wasn't going to help her today and disappeared into the kitchen. Good, the less time he spent with her the better.

He did his best to ignore her when she returned for more dishes and studied how much wallpaper they had to strip. He should go across the street and see if the chandelier he ordered had arrived, but it could wait. The sooner they were done with the dining room, the sooner he could start working upstairs, and then he'd hardly see Dora at all.

When she returned a third time, she worked slowly,

picking up pieces of silverware one by one. Was she lingering?

Phileas turned away and tried not to think about her. Hard to do when his heart was hammering and his gut was tight. He wanted to hold her with every fiber of his being, but it was not to be. He had no choice now but to return to England, no thanks to his brothers. But he couldn't let himself become bitter over their falling in love with some of the locals. He'd never seen them so happy. And there was still a chance that Sterling or one of the others would return for good. Who knew what the future held?

He got back to work, and unfortunately, that meant going into the kitchen to get some hot water to get the old wallpaper off. He wondered if McSweeny would boot him out, but that didn't bother him. What did is how he'd react to Dora if he got too close to her. Would he be able to stand it?

In the kitchen, McSweeny was washing dishes while Dora dried. She gave Phileas a quick glance as he headed for the stove, then quickly looked away.

"I need the kettle." He took a dishrag and lifted it.

"Needs water," McSweeny said. "I can make sure there's plenty so you can get that paper off."

"I appreciate that." He glanced at Dora as he took the kettle outside to the pump. She didn't say a word.

As soon as he started pumping water, he relaxed a little. When he was in the same room with her, he could scarce breathe of late. He was wondering if he'd make it through the day. But so long as he could keep his distance, he might manage it.

He brought the kettle to the stove. "I'll be back for this." Without another word, he left the kitchen and returned to Oliver. Conrad and Irving were with him. "Well?" Conrad said. "Did you speak to her?"

"No." He sighed in relief, as if he'd just escaped a wild beast. "She's doing dishes with McSweeny."

"Fine fellow," Irving said. "I hope he stays."

Phileas shook his head. "I'm not sure Dora will like that."

"I didn't mean here." Irving waved at their surroundings. "I mean in town. If he cooks at the saloon, then people can have the option of dining out. Not only that, so will Dora's hotel guests. They wouldn't have to dine here if they didn't want to."

"But would that be taking business away from her?" Oliver asked.

"No," Phileas said sagely. "It would help her. Meals are included in the price of a room. If not everyone is eating here, then she doesn't have to prepare as much food, thus saving money. She'll make more income."

Oliver nodded in understanding. "I see. So Mr. McSweeny using the saloon as a restaurant is a good thing."

"It is," Conrad said. "And good for the town." He smiled. "You know what we have to do?"

Irving nodded. "Convince McSweeny to stay."

"Exactly." Conrad nudged Phileas with an elbow. "How are you holding up, old chap?"

He put a hand over his heart. "I'll make it."

"You sure about that?" Irving asked.

"I've no choice, do I?" Phileas headed for the nearest wall and peeled what he could. Part of him was growing resentful, and he knew if he let it sink in, he'd go back to England with a chip on his shoulder. He didn't want that. Though part of him didn't want to go at all.

Chapter Nineteen

Dora sat across the dining table from Alma and Letty. Cassie sat beside her. "Well, what are you going to do?"

She looked Cassie's way, unblinking. "I'm not sure. Get through the next couple of weeks, then deal with what happens next."

There was a knock at the door. It opened and Jean poked her head in. "Sorry I'm late." She stepped into Alma's parlor and joined them. "What did I miss?"

Letty gave Dora a sympathetic look. "Dora's having a hard time."

"So I've heard." Jean smiled at her, then sat.

Dora had no idea who told who what was happening and didn't care. She needed help, but was it already too late? "I'm sorry if this all seems confusing."

Alma gave her a heartfelt smile. "We understand. You don't want to fall in love. But how do you do that? I'm afraid I'm not much help. I've never fallen in love before."

"But we have." Cassie looked at Jean and Letty. "I asked myself over and over again what might happen if I fell in love with Conrad. I didn't want to. He was a flirt, for one. But when he didn't flirt much with me, I had more of a chance to observe him."

Dora sighed. "And you fell in love with what you saw?"

Cassie nodded. "Yes. The more time I spent with him."

Letty glanced around the table. "Dora is trying to avoid a broken heart, so all we have to do is make sure she's not around Phileas. With Mr. McSweeny cooking, she can be with one of us and can avoid having meals with him."

Cassie stared at Dora. "What would be so bad about..."

"She can't," Letty cut in. "*He* can't."

"Fall in love?" Cassie sat back in her chair arms crossed. "I don't see what would be..."

Letty kicked her under the table.

Dora watched them a moment then tried to ignore them. All they were doing at this point was trying to ease her already broken heart. She didn't know when it happened. Maybe if she'd enlisted her friends' help sooner, she wouldn't be in this predicament. Sooner or later Phileas and Oliver would leave, and she could go back to normal. But then, would things ever be normal again?

A better question was, did she want them to be? Before the Darlings came to town, she had no business, the town was drying up, and no one wanted to come to Apple Blossom after the incident. People from Virginia City to Bozeman thought outlaws were still about and didn't want to risk life and limb to go from one place to the other. Instead, they circled around Apple Blossom like it was some sort of disease.

She took a shuddering breath. Was she wasting everyone's time? Perhaps, but she didn't want to face what was coming by herself either. "Just... keep me away from him, that's all I ask."

"Sure, we can do that," Cassie said. "Do you want Etta to help?"

"Etta?" Dora fought an eye roll. "She hardly leaves the blacksmith's shop and livery. She won't be any help."

Letty reached across the table and took her hand. "We'll do our best." She looked at the others. "Won't we?"

They nodded their agreement.

Before Dora could thank them, they heard the faint sound of the bell over the door downstairs in the storefront. "It's time I got back to work," Alma said. She left the table.

"That goes for me too." Cassie got up, as did Jean.

Dora was the last to leave as Alma headed downstairs, the rest following.

She closed the door behind her and headed down herself. When she reached the storefront, her friends were lined up behind the counter staring at Phileas. She gasped as her heart leaped.

"Dora!" Alma shoved her way past the others, took her arms, and ushered her through the door to the back. "Remember that bolt of fabric I wanted to show you?"

Dora gave her a blank stare. "Why are you talking so loud?"

Alma rolled her eyes. "Here it is. Take a look and tell me what you think." She narrowed her eyes, then hissed, "I'm keeping you away from Phileas." She tossed her head at the storefront. "Stay here." She turned around and went through the door, closing it behind her.

Dora sighed as her shoulders slumped. Well, she did ask for their help, and they were giving it.

Unable to help herself, she went to the door, put her ear against it, and heard Phileas ask about the chandelier. She'd forgotten he'd ordered one and began to look around the large storeroom. She didn't see one anywhere. Had it even arrived?

She found a chair near the stairs leading up to Alma's living quarters, sat, then buried her face in her hands. She was suddenly tired, as if she carried the weight of the world on her shoulders. But all it was, was the knowledge that Phileas and Oliver would be gone soon and now she was suffering the same thing her friends did.

The difference was, there was nothing she could do about her situation. It didn't matter if she fell for Phileas or not—he was still leaving. She didn't have all the details other than someone had to return to explain what had happened to the rest of the Darlings. Poor Phileas. Would his parents be upset? Would they blame him for his brothers staying behind? Letty, or was it Cassie, let slip something about the brothers being disowned by the parents...

She sat up, wiped her eyes and stared straight ahead. "No wonder he has to go back. He's doing it for his brothers." She closed her eyes, letting the thought sink in. Phileas was doing a noble thing, trying to protect them and see that they still got a little something when their parents passed one day. But she was sure they would visit England with their American wives at some point. Phileas' job would be to prepare their parents for that day.

In the meantime, she imagined Phileas and Oliver would have to work extra hard on the family farm to get their harvests in and do whatever else needed to be done. She wasn't a farmer, so she didn't know how much work that entailed for them. But from the sound of it, the Darlings had a large farm, and it made her wonder how the work was getting done while the six brothers were here in America.

In the meantime, she had to do what she could to avoid interacting with him too much. The sooner he was gone, the better.

She waited by the door and listened. She could still

hear Phileas speaking to Alma and the others. Why hadn't Cassie and Letty left yet?

With a sigh, she contemplated going back upstairs to Alma's dining room and making herself a cup of tea. Who knew how long Phileas would stay?

Instead, she sat on the staircase, put her chin in her hands and waited for Phileas to leave. She didn't hear him ask after her, so maybe he didn't care that she wasn't at the hotel. Maybe he didn't care whether or not she was around. If so, this was all one-sided. But hadn't she known it was all along? So what if kissed her on the cheek the other day? It meant nothing. British gentlemen probably did that sort of thing all the time.

She waited a few minutes more, heard nothing coming from up front, and unable to stand it, marched into the storefront—and right into Phileas.

"Oof!"

Dora stared at him in horror. "Oh, dear."

"Oh, dear," Letty, Cassie and Jean echoed.

He looked the four over, his eyes settling on Dora. "I say, but have you been back there the whole time?"

She tried to wipe the shocked look off her face by wiggling her nose. "Er... we were having tea earlier."

His eyes roamed over her. Not in an "I don't believe you" sort of way. No, this was the look of a man who hadn't seen someone he cared about for a long time, and now they stood before him. But why was he looking at her like that? She'd seen him at breakfast.

Phileas took a step back. "I say, but are the four of

you in the habit of congregating on the upper floor of the general store? This is the first time I've seen you do it."

Dora exchanged a quick look with the others. "We meet now and then to visit. You're just used to seeing us do it at the hotel."

His face screwed up in thought before he smiled. "Yes, you're quite right. I have seen you conversing in the hotel kitchen." He sighed. "Seems McSweeny has taken it over. "

Dora shrugged. "There are worse things. If he's willing to cook for a time, who am I to argue? You told me yourself I should take a break."

"I did, didn't I?" He swallowed hard, then motioned toward the door. "I should be going." His eyes lingered on her a moment longer. "Well, off I go." He took one step back, two steps.

Dora fought the urge to follow. When he did finally turn and walk out the door, her heart ached and her limbs became heavy, as if someone had just covered her in chains. She didn't understand why she would feel this way, but figured she wouldn't have to put up with it for long. As soon as Phileas and Oliver left Apple Blossom, she could have a proper broken heart and all that went with it.

Phileas crossed the street to the hotel. Seeing her burst through the door and headlong into him was the highlight of his day. He'd wanted to wrap her in his arms and never let go. Egads, but this was bad. If he didn't get a hold of himself, his family's legacy could be lost. Okay, not lost, but it would certainly cause a lot of problems if he never went back to England.

"Where have you been?" Conrad asked when he entered the lobby. He looked at his empty hands. "No chandelier?"

"It's not here yet." He went into the dining room and sat at the nearest table. "I ran into Dora. Or rather, she ran into me."

Irving shook his head in dismay. "This isn't boding well for you, is it?"

Oliver sat next to him. "What can we do?"

Phileas ran both hands through his hair. "What you should have been doing. Keeping me away from Dora."

Conrad chuckled. "And then you had to go and run into her." He looked at the others. "I think love is in him."

"But Conrad," Oliver said, not bothering to hide the worry in his voice. "If Phileas falls, what happens to the estate and title?"

Irving stepped forward. "Who's to say? None of us knows what's going to happen. Sterling could wake up one day and pack up his things and head for England. Any of us could, for that matter."

"What are you saying?" Phileas asked.

Irving paced. "That things aren't as dire as we've been making them out to be. We've each been so wrapped up in our own little affairs of the heart, none of us has taken the time to think about other options or alternatives."

"He's right," Conrad said. "We're trying to do things the way they've always been done."

Oliver stopped Irving's pacing. "But if all of you stay and I go back, what then?"

"Do you want the title?" Phileas asked.

Oliver shrugged. "I couldn't say. I've just finished school. I've not had to deal with any of it yet."

Conrad patted him on the shoulder. "Don't worry. Father will bend you to his will soon enough."

Oliver gulped. "Don't you mean mold me?"

"No, brother, I mean bend." Conrad let go of his shoulder and sat on the other side of Phileas. "Father wants us to run the estate the way it always has been. Now if Phileas agrees with him, then by all means, he should go back to England and see it done while the rest of us live out our lives in this quaint little town and make the best of it."

Phileas stared at him a moment. "What do you mean?"

"He's saying you and Oliver should have it all," Irving said. "We made our choice to get married once the town gets a new preacher and stay the course here."

"True," Conrad said. "Which means if we're not helping you with the estate, then you two should have it. After all, if you're doing all the work, then you should be the ones to reap the rewards."

Phileas ran his hand through his hair again and took a shuddering breath. "I'm not sure I agree with that."

"The four of us have discussed it," Irving said.

Phileas nodded, still thinking. It was a fair trade, and if any of them were ever in trouble, he would of course help them out. "And if it comes down to Oliver?"

"Then we'll do what we can to help him," Irving said. "But the same rule applies. If he's there and we're all here, then he should reap the benefits and rewards of his labor. Besides, if he's the only one there to put up with Mother, he'll more than deserve it."

They chuckled at the joke, but Phileas was still unsettled. What it came down to was two questions. Was he in love with Dora or not? And if so, what was he going to do about it?

But that wasn't his only problem. What if he was in love with her, and she didn't care a whit about him? Simply put, there would be no reason to stay. He and Oliver would return, deal with their parents and do what they could to run the estate and prepare to take it over one day. Something easier said than done considering its size.

But first things first. Was he in love with Dora? He remembered the way she looked when she ran into him earlier, her eyes slightly widened in surprise and her hair falling in wisps around her face. It was as if time had stopped, and all he could see was her. He couldn't deny the pull he felt towards her, but he was still unsure of what to do about it.

He needed a walk to clear his head. After excusing himself, he headed out the door and tried to analyze his feelings. Yes, he enjoyed her company and their conversations, but was that enough to be in love? The other night he thought he was, but love was more than a feeling. A lot more.

But what about her? Did she feel the same way? Did she realize what love was?

By the time he reached the bank, Phileas decided he needed to ask her. He headed back to the hotel, his heart racing with nerves. When he entered, it was through the back of the building, and he went straight to the kitchen. But it wasn't Dora standing at the stove, but McSweeny. "Oh, dash it all." He rubbed his chin a few times. Hmm ... maybe talking to McSweeny would help him sort out his thoughts.

"Ah, Mr. Darling," McSweeny said, glancing his way. "What can I get for you?"

Phileas shook his head. "Actually, I was hoping to talk to you. It's about Dora."

McSweeny's eyebrows shot up in surprise. "Dora? Well, I suppose I can't blame you. The girl's got spunk."

Phileas grinned despite himself. "Yes, she does. But I'm not sure what to do about it. I think I might be..." He trailed off, unable to put into words what he was feeling. Why was he telling this to a complete stranger anyway? Other than he'd get an unbiased opinion.

"In love with her?" McSweeny finished for him. "Yes, I think you might be too."

Phileas was taken aback. "How do you know?"

McSweeny chuckled. "I've seen the way you look at her. And believe me, I know that look. I've worn it myself." He stopped stirring a pot and squinted at him. "So, what are you gonna do about it?"

Phileas went to the table and sank into the nearest chair. "Express my love and wait for her to reject me, I suppose."

"What?! That's no way to win the heart of a woman."

Phileas chuckled low in his throat. "And I suppose you can tell me what is?"

McSweeny straightened, squinted at him over the rim of his spectacles and grinned. "I can."

Chapter Twenty

Two days later Dora took in the hotel's dining room. It was in shambles. Everything near the walls had been moved to the center of the room. The two tables they used to dine at were now closer to the kitchen door, and the sideboard in the room had been moved there too. Mainly because it was in use.

Mr. McSweeny brought out another platter of food and set it down. "Miss Jones, do you need something?"

"No, just... looking." Strips of wallpaper were crumpled up in buckets, and there were bits of debris here and there. All in all, though, Phileas and his brothers had the walls free of the old paper and could start on the new tomorrow. She'd been spending time with her friends, trying to stay away from Phileas, and enjoyed her break from the hotel's kitchen. But she could only do that for so long. She wanted to check on things and make sure Mr. McSweeny hadn't destroyed it.

She watched him go through the swinging door and followed. She gasped when she entered. "Oh, my..."

He turned to her and smiled. "I hope you don't mind. I took the liberty of straightening up a few things."

The room sparkled, it was so clean. "Not at all." She felt a twinge of embarrassment, but it was quickly gone. "What did you make for dinner?"

"I thought your guests could dish themselves up, then take their food out back to eat."

"What? But there's nothing back there but grass and patches of dirt."

"And an orchard. There are folded blankets stacked on a crate by the back door."

She smiled. Why did she never think of doing something like this? "So a picnic dinner."

"No, we're dining outside. I made roast beef with potatoes, onions and carrots. We'll also have salad and then a dessert. Sometimes eating in a unique environment makes an ordinary meal extraordinary."

Dora smiled. "I suppose it does." She didn't know what else to say. He'd already gone through all the trouble to prepare this, so he should be allowed to see it through. "I'll join you shortly." She left the dining room, went to her quarters and sat on her loveseat for a while. So far she'd avoided Phileas by spending time elsewhere, but she had nowhere to go tonight so here she was, trying to figure out a way to eat alone.

She sighed and went to her window. She saw one of the smaller dining room tables outside, covered with glasses and pitchers of what looked like iced tea, stacks of napkins and silverware. If she wasn't so miserable, this would be fun. Instead, she'd be near Phileas, and she was going to have to think of how to not get into a conversation with him.

She sighed. Why did this have to be so hard? Why couldn't she have been satisfied with having Phileas as a friend? Why did she have to fall in love?

She wiped away a tear, stood, then left her rooms. The Darlings were already filing into the dining room. She heard the men comment and noticed that Letty and Jean were among them. Would Cassie be joining them too? She hoped so. For one, the couples would sit together. That left her with either Flint and Lacey, or Oliver. With any luck, he'd sit with Phileas while she ate with the children.

She watched everyone line up near the sideboard. Mr. McSweeny began passing plates out and directing everyone where to start. As each began moving through the line filling their plates, she noticed there was no sign of Phileas. Where was he?

"Good evening."

She almost choked. Land sakes, he was right behind her. She turned around as a chill went up her spine and blinked in disbelief. He was stunning. "Wh-what are you wearing?"

He smiled then brushed at his suit. "Normal attire for a gentleman."

She looked him over. While the others were wearing

their everyday clothes, Phileas looked like he was dressed for an evening out at a play or opera. He wasn't wearing a tuxedo, but around here he was definitely in the equivalent. "Why?"

His smile was warm, inviting. "Because tonight is special, Dora."

She made a face and backed up a step. "What for?"

He looked into her eyes as he drew closer. "I have an announcement to make."

"Are you hoping your clothes will make it easier for everyone to take?" Dora closed her eyes and turned away. She shouldn't have said that. "I'm sorry. It's just that I know you're leaving, and I also know your brothers want you to stay." She faced him again. "I think what you're doing for them is kind and selfless."

He smiled gently. "You think I'm kind and selfless?"

"I do." She backed up again. Being near him was downright intoxicating and if she didn't move away, she might not be able to stand much longer.

"Dora," he whispered. "Is something wrong?"

Everything's wrong! she wanted to scream. But there was no point. Phileas was different and did things the same way. He was announcing his departure date, no doubt. The dining room was coming along, and she'd noticed Sterling and Irving speaking with Mr. Hawthorne. Were the Darlings planning on splitting up to help different individuals and get things done that way? Had Phileas spoken to them about finishing her rooms upstairs?

"Dora?" he whispered.

She closed her eyes, took a breath, then let it out. "What?"

He leaned down to whisper in her ear. "The food's getting cold."

Dora took a shuddering breath, nodded, then headed for the sideboard.

Phileas took a deep breath as he watched Dora cross the dining room. She wore a white blouse, a light blue skirt and sash, and her hair was pulled back at the crown, the rest long and flowing. It was a typical look for her, but today she took his breath away. Amazing what making up your mind could do. Was he terrified to express his feelings for her? Most definitely. Would he still go through with it? Of course.

Vernon McSweeny was a mystery. The squinting old man could cook alongside the best of them, and his tales of traveling the world were astounding. So many adventures! What he wouldn't give to have one like Vernon. He'd been to the deepest darkest jungles of Africa and India alike. Climbed the Swiss Alps, been to Germany, England, France, Scotland. He'd dined with dukes, duchesses and even a king and queen! What a life!

But it was how he did it that amazed Phileas and his brothers. Vernon McSweeny didn't travel round the world like some famed explorer. He cooked his way from one place to another. The man might be blind as a bat, but his nose made up for it. He could tell what would work in a dish by smell alone. He called it a freak of nature; Phileas and his brothers called it a gift. And now here he was in Apple Blossom with his long-time friend Captain Stanley, cooking for a bunch of Englishmen and a few townsfolk and looking for a place to settle.

He also had a nose for love. Phileas was in love with Dora, and McSweeny told him to take the risk, to profess his deepest most feelings and see what happened. After he thought about it, Phileas decided, why not? Depending on how she responded, he'd know what to do next. So, he spoke to his brothers, told them he was in love with Dora (despite their best efforts to keep him from being so) and asked for their advice. They came to an agreement, and he would make the announcement. But first, he had to speak to Dora. If she had no feelings for him, then so be it. He would return to England with Oliver. But if she did...

"Are you going to eat?"

He smiled at her then looked around. They were the only two left in the dining room. He joined her at the sideboard. "By Jove, will you look at all of this?"

"Mr. McSweeny said he was making roast beef and some vegetables. But this is so much more."

Phileas nodded. There was roast beef all right, along with mashed potatoes, glazed carrots, salad, corn, fried apples, and gravy for the meat and potatoes. "One would think we're dining with royalty."

"I told him not to use my best china, but he didn't listen." She glanced at him, gulped, then looked away.

He stood close behind her. "Dora, there's something I need to talk to you about."

She stiffened. "Does this have to do with your announcement that you're leaving?"

He smiled. She didn't know she was the determining factor. "Yes."

Her shoulders slumped. "Can it wait until after I eat?"

Phileas leaned down. "No."

She went still. "Wh-why not?"

He licked his lips. He wanted to kiss her but didn't dare. "Because my announcement depends on your answer."

She faced him, the only thing between them the plate of food in her hand. "What's the question?"

He noted the rise and fall of her chest. Her breaths were shaky and growing shorter. He took the plate from her. "Before we join the others, I need to know something."

She looked agonized. "Must you?" She shut her eyes tight. "Must you even speak to me? Do you have any idea what I've been through these past days? Any idea at all?"

Her voice rose in pitch, and he noted that too. She was growing more upset by the second, just as McSweeny had predicted. He smiled. "He really can sniff out love."

Her eyes popped wide. "What?"

Phileas smiled and rubbed the back of his neck. He

was nervous and rightly so. He'd prepared himself for rejection, but this? "Dora, I'm about to do something that will affect not only me but my brothers as well."

"What?" She looked skeptical, and like she couldn't wait to get away from him.

He set her plate on the sideboard, then looked her in the eyes. "Dora Jones, I think you're the most beautiful, wonderful, generous woman I've ever met. It has honored me to work on your hotel."

She quirked a smile. "Th-that's it, then? You're proud to have worked with me?"

"Yes." He took her arms and pulled her against him. "Oh, and by the way, I love you." Phileas kissed her then and didn't hold back.

&

Dora didn't know what had happened. One minute she was about to laugh hysterically (who wouldn't after Phileas' little speech?) then the next he was kissing her! But wait, what did he say before he made her lose her mind? She tried to push him away and, lo-and-behold, succeeded. "What? What are you doing?!"

His face fell, and he sighed. "So that's it, then." He nodded to himself before he straightened and bowed. He looked into her eyes before he brushed a finger across her cheek.

She wiped away the tears that fell. "What are you doing?"

He lowered his hand. "Can you forgive me?"

"For k-kissing me?" She swallowed hard. "Why?"

"Because it's clear you did not wish to be kissed. I apologize." He sighed, then headed for the lobby.

Her heart in her throat, she ran after him. "Phileas, wait!"

He stopped but didn't turn around. "Yes?"

"What did you say?" She caught up to him and took his arm. "What did you just tell me?" Her lower lip trembled, and tears stung her eyes but she didn't care. "Please."

He turned, gazed at her with a warm smile, then tucked a finger under her chin. "I told you this." And he kissed her again.

Her knees went weak and buckled. He held her against him to support her but didn't break the kiss. Instead, he deepened it.

Dora thought she'd died and gone to Heaven. Could it be? H-he loved her?! But... how did she not see it? They were friends, he kissed her on the cheek one day, but that was it...

He didn't give her time to think as the kiss deepened further. The words he spoke earlier were clear. Phileas Darling loved her.

When he broke the kiss, he held her close. "My darling Dora, I have to ask you, do you have any ounce of feelings..."

"Yes!" She looked at him, eyes wide. "You're asking if I love you. I do!"

His smile grew as his eyes locked with hers. He sighed in relief, kissed the top of her head, and continued to hold her. "What I do now is for us."

She trembled. The shock of his profession of love, not to mention his kisses, were overwhelming. "Phileas," she whispered. "What are you going to do?"

He smiled again. "I'm going to go out there and announce that I'm staying on."

Her eyes rounded. "Staying?"

"Yes, darling," he whispered. "Because I've fallen in love, you see, and I cannot go back without my wife at my side."

Her mouth moved but nothing came out at first. "Wife?"

His eyes roamed her face for a moment before settling on her mouth. "You'll go as my wife, darling. Or I won't go at all." He let her go, got down on one knee, and took her hands in his. "Dora Jones, I am Phileas Sebastian Darlington, the fourth son of the Viscount Darlington of Sussex. Will you marry me?"

She stared at him. "Darling*ton*?"

He nodded. "It was safer for us to travel under that name."

"I don't understand, what's a viscount?"

"It's a title."

"But... you're a farmer."

"I'm the son of a viscount who has a lot of tenant farmers." He gave her hands a squeeze. "Dash it all, woman, will you marry me or not?"

Tears filled her eyes. She didn't care what a viscount was or even if she had to go to England. "Yes! Yes, I'll marry you!"

He stood, pulled her into his arms and kissed her again. This time she relaxed against him and kissed him back. Her head was swimming with happiness, and she still had lots of questions, but for now, the only question she cared about was the one she'd just answered.

When he broke the kiss this time, he held her a moment. "I'm sorry I waited. But I had to be sure, and we had to talk about things, and McSweeny got a hold of me..."

"Mr. McSweeny? What does he have to do with any of this?"

He grinned. "You have no idea. Suffice to say, when one is facing a deadline the tendency to not know one's feelings is high."

"You didn't know if you were in love with me?"

He held up one hand and brought his index finger and thumb together. "I had an inkling."

She smiled. "So you love me. I said yes." She bit her lip. "I should say I love you too."

"Then please do."

She looked into his eyes. "I love you, Phileas—for a long time, I think. You're right, a deadline does make things confusing. I tried so hard to stay away from you these past few days."

"Yes, I noticed you had help."

She smiled. "Was it that obvious?"

"Was mine?"

Dora laughed. "You mean, you..."

"Oliver and the rest of my brothers were supposed to be aiding me, but... well, they slacked in their duties."

"I'm glad they did." She stood on tiptoe and kissed him.

He broke it, smiled, then nodded at the lobby. "I need to make my announcement."

She nodded. "All right."

He escorted her outside where the others were seated on blankets on the grass, eating. All eyes were suddenly upon them as Sterling got to his feet. "Well, brother? Will you tell us now?"

Phileas took a deep breath. "Everyone, I've decided I will return to England to see to *our* affairs. And I will do it with my wife." He looked at Dora and smiled. "That is, if she'll still have me."

She reached up and cupped his face in her hand. "Always and to the ends of the Earth."

He took her hand, kissed it, then faced his brothers. "We will be your advocates, Dora and I, but we will not return to England until I see fit. We have work to do here. I'm sending a message with Captain Stanley to take to the telegraph office in Virginia City. It will let Mother and Father know we are all fine and that we're staying a while longer." He smiled at them. "A long while for some."

Oliver looked at the others, then raised his hand. "But... Phileas, what about me?"

"You will travel with us, if you like, or you can stay here. The choice is yours. But once we are all wed, we will begin working out how we will split up the duties of the estate, the care of our parents, all of it." He smiled at Sterling. "After all, the next Viscount Darlington is going to need our help."

Letty gasped. "Sterling?"

"I'm the eldest, love, the next in line to inherit. We decided to leave things as they are as far as all that goes, but if working together, I won't have to be there all the time. We can split the duties up amongst us and each spend a couple months out of the year in England."

Oliver raised his hand again. "But, Sterling, what about me?"

Sterling laughed. "Ollie, if you find yourself a wife in England, that's all well and good. And who knows, you may find yourself a wife here."

"Don't worry," Phileas said. "You won't have to face Mother and Father alone. You can marry a woman of your choosing, not theirs."

Oliver's shoulders slumped in relief. "Thank goodness."

Cassie set her plate aside. "But...I can't leave Apple Blossom."

"We've worked that out too," Sterling said. "Two of us will step in as acting sheriff and deputy when it's Conrad's turn to go. But let's not talk about this now. Let's enjoy our meal and share in Phileas and Dora's happiness." He smiled at them then raised his glass of iced tea. "To Phileas and Dora!"

Everyone raised their glass. "To Phileas and Dora!"

Dora wiped a tear away as she watched them toast. She'd expected none of this and was becoming overwhelmed with happiness. She noticed there was no sign of Mr. McSweeny and figured he must be in the kitchen. Part of her nagged at her to help him while the rest of her told that part to be quiet. She just got engaged to a handsome Englishman with a talent for wallpapering. The Darlings weren't who anyone thought they were, and she was going to get to go to England. It was all too wonderful. But more so was the man at her side. She'd work out the particulars of running off to England later.

She stood on tiptoe to whisper in his ear. "I love you."

He bent to her. "I love you too."

She smiled, then whispered, "I take it no one else but those gathered here know who you are."

"Quite right."

"Does it matter?"

"For now, yes."

She nodded then looked him in the eyes. "I trust you."

Phileas smiled. "I know, my love." He kissed her then, and for Dora, he was all that mattered.

The End

About the Author

Kit Morgan has written for fun all of her life. Whether she's writing contemporary or historical romance, her whimsical stories are fun, inspirational, sweet and clean, and depict a strong sense of family and community. Raised by a homicide detective, one would think she'd write suspense, (and yes, she plans to get around to those eventually, cozy mysteries too!) but Kit likes fun and romantic westerns! Kit resides in the beautiful Pacific Northwest in a little log cabin on Clear Creek, after which her fictional town that appears in many of her books is named.

Want to get in on the fun?

Find out about new releases, cover reveals, bonus content, fun times and more! Sign up for Kit's newsletter at www.authorkitmorgan.com